A Novel

KNOCK KNOCK

STEVEN T. THOMAS

© 2023 by Horror Haven Books
Cover design by rebecacovers on Fiverr © 2023
Internal design by Steven T. Thomas

All rights reserved. No part of this book may be reproduced in any form or by any electronic or mechanical means including information storage and retrieval systems---except in the case of brief quotations embodied in critical articles or reviews---without permission in writing from its author, Steven T. Thomas.

The characters and events portrayed in this book are fictitious or are used fictitiously. Any similarity to real persons, living or dead, is purely coincidental and not intended by the author.
All brand names and product names used in this book are trademarks, registered trademarks, or trade names of their respective holders. Steven T. Thomas is not associated with any product or vendor in this book.

Printed and bound in the United States of America.

Horror Haven Books
3237 Muir Rd.
Dryden, MI 48428
www.authorsteventhomas.com

To Grandma.
You taught me I could do anything.

KNOCK KNOCK

PROLOGUE

DELILAH CARNEY

As cliche as it sounds, it was a dark and stormy night—but this wasn't just any dark and stormy night. The rain was pounding on the ground hard and fast and the wind whipped around me like I was caught in a tornado—at least sixty mile per hour gusts. It pushed me around as I got out of the car and attempted to close the door. It felt like I was fighting for my life just pushing the metal panel and making sure it latched properly.

Cooper and I had just enjoyed a nice evening out; he used to take me out for these things he called "friend dates." He is, by far, the best friend I've ever had—sweet, caring and enjoyable to be around. He treated me to a night out and we went to the theater to see Ready Or Not, which is a fantastic movie, then took me out to dinner. I had a really nice time with him; until I got home, that is.

As we sat at dinner talking about life and what we planned on doing for the rest of our lives, Cooper proposed something that I wasn't too fond of, but agreed anyway, because again, he's my best friend and I wanted to support him. He suggested we start a podcast and I was a bit surprised by his willingness to put himself out there like that. Cooper, my sweet, introverted best friend, wanted to start a podcast and speak in front of potentially thousands of people. I agreed, though, and we discussed what we would cover. It was simple for us to pick, really: True Crime.

I'd always been a true crime and horror fanatic and he liked the suspense that comes with thrillers, so it only made sense that that was the route we took. We decided after that night we would get together again soon and start planning for what was to come. He didn't waste any time—he wanted out of his crappy retail job at

Best Buy and I knew that was his plan all along: to try to run a podcast full time and make enough money to cover the bills.

As I closed my door, I could see his opening and he jumped out of the vehicle as quickly as he could. Cooper ran to my side with the umbrella he had stashed in his backseat, quickly opened it, and ushered me to the front door of my parent's house. What a gentleman. If he wasn't such a great friend, I'd have considered dating him, but I didn't want to risk losing him through the drama that comes with dating someone.

Even with the umbrella opened above, the rain still pelted us hard as the wind pushed it to come down sideways. With our vision impaired, we didn't even notice the front door to my house was left ajar until we stepped onto the patio. Rain was pouring into the foyer and flooding the tile floor in the entryway. The two of us exchanged a look of concern as we stepped in. Before coming in, he closed the umbrella and left it at the front door.

Our feet sloshed and the carpet beyond the tile squished under us as we stepped around trying to find a dry spot to take off our shoes.

"Mom? Dad?" I yelled, but received no response.

"Darcy?" I yelled, but even my sister didn't respond to me.

Cooper had a puzzled look on his face, like a detective trying to riddle out a mystery. We exchanged looks of confusion and fear, then he spoke up, "I'll go upstairs and look around, you look around down here."

As I searched downstairs, I found no trace of my family even being there this evening. But with my mom being the way she was, they wouldn't have gone out in the storm. Even at that, I knew they were there when I left. I waved them goodbye as I ran outside to meet Cooper.

As I rounded the corner into the kitchen, it looked like a bomb went off in the room—cabinets and cupboards were open, knives had fallen to the floor, and even the refrigerator was open. I took a closer look at the stainless steel door with the ice and filtered water dispenser; there was something out of place dripping off the ledge. I inched my way toward it and noticed instantly the ruby-red liquid that pooled. Out of sheer instinct and panic I put my finger in it. Blood.

My heart raced and pounded in my chest almost as hard as the rain hitting the roof. I looked down to the floor and found droplets of blood not only under the fridge, but leading to the living room so I followed them.

I turned the corner into the living room and let out a blood curdling scream as I saw what was before me. I heard pounding upstairs as Cooper ran like a bat out of hell to my side. His eyes widened as he saw them: my family laying on the floor covered in blood and stab wounds. He grabbed onto me and tried to shield me from the sight but I fought his embrace and ran to my dad's side. Though I knew it wouldn't do any good, I started to shake him and yelled "Dad" through my sobbing.

I looked up at Cooper, who was standing behind me looking white as a ghost, unsure of what to do for me right then. The look on his face showed me a mix of compassion, fear and uncertainty. He walked up, grabbed me, and tried to pull me away from the puddle of blood soaking into the white carpet. I followed him as he pulled me out of the room, and, as we entered back into the foyer, we both looked up and gasped at the sight in front of us.

Right above the front door to my house, dripping down the wall, there were words written, not in pen or marker, but in blood. The words were a calling card and, as I took it, a warning. We stared at the artwork with mouths agape. The writing looked like it was done with haste—sloppily thrown up on the wall and this monster used my family's blood to write it. As the realization hit, so did nausea, and I had to do everything in my power to fight back the vomit crawling up my throat as I read the words:

Knock Knock.

PART 1

CHAPTER 1

COOPER COBB

THREE YEARS LATER

"I think we need to start going live on Friday nights," I say as Delilah and I sit in the Coffee Station dining room.

The Milan Coffee Station is the place where we sit and discuss what we will be doing for the next episode and how we can improve the show. I don't really know how it came about but one day we decided to start coming here when we are brainstorming—for some reason it just puts us in the right mindset for it.

My name is Cooper Cobb. I run a show called "The Knock Knock Podcast" with my best friend, Delilah. We started it two years ago as a simple True Crime podcast covering different crimes each week as everyone else does. But as we grew, so did the show. Now we cover one topic and one topic only: The Knock Knock Killer.

The Knock Knock Killer was a serial killer from our area in Milan, Ohio. Why was he called the Knock Knock Killer? His typical M.O. would be to go to seemingly random homes, knock two times and wait for someone to answer the door. Once they did, he would force his way into the house and murder the entire family. He is responsible for six family murders from 2016 until 2019, but his rampage ended about three years ago.

I think the worst of all of his crimes was the second to last family that he murdered. I may be biased on it, but it was the Carney family; Delilah's mother, father, and sister. She wasn't home at the time and is the only living survivor of the Knock Knock Killer. I hate to say she was in the right place at the right time, but she was. My best friend survived, though somedays it feels like she wishes she hadn't. It's been a tough journey for her mentally, but these days, she's doing much better and creating the podcast is almost therapeutic to her.

Was he caught? No. Our local police force is about as useful as tits on a boar hog. They closed the case three years ago due to a lack of evidence and that's what led Delilah and I to where we are now. Our show is all about the evidence, hoping someone comes forward with information, hoping someone knows something. We want to solve the case.

Can you imagine? An online weekly radio show solving a case that the police couldn't. The thought is laughable, but we are determined to be the first ones to figure it out.

"Live shows?" She asks, as if she didn't hear me.

"Live shows," I say back, confirming.

Delilah thinks about it for a moment, then agrees with me. I knew she might see it my way. We've never tried a live show, but the more I thought about it, the more I thought it would probably be a good way to showcase us, bring in more listeners, and engage the current listeners we already have.

"What will we do on these live shows?"

"I'm thinking we save all of the big stuff for the recorded episodes and focus on the listeners on the live shows, maybe do a Q&A; things like that," I say.

"Yeah, I'm down, that could be fun," she says, "but is Infinite okay with that?"

"Already talked to them."

Infinite Podcasting is our distribution company. As the show grew in popularity, we started getting noticed by the companies in the industry that represent podcasters and Infinite approached us about coming on to their network of shows. They distribute and represent some of the biggest names in the True Crime podcasting market and we didn't have to chase them down. They practically begged us to come aboard, so we negotiated a little bit and signed the paperwork. With a distribution deal comes studio time, which they pay for. They do take a small cut of the advertising revenue to cover a portion of the costs, but other than that, we get paid for all of the ads that we run.

We are going to have to travel to Michigan soon. They've decided they want us to start touring which, of course, through more negotiation, we obliged. They want to do a trial run in front of a live audience at the Fox Theatre in Detroit. I couldn't say why they chose Detroit of all places—I'm not too keen on going there from what I've heard about the city, but when they say jump, we have to jump.

"Well, then let's do this," Delilah says, "when do we start?"

I hadn't thought that far ahead. When should we start?

"Do you think we could be prepared to start next Friday?" I ask.

"I think we can pull that off."

It never took too much fighting between us to make something work. We've been friends for a long time and we understand one another. Hell, we even took the leap to move in together and we've been living that life for about three and a half years. It's strictly platonic, though, and there's never been any sort of sexual tension or talks of a relationship between us—that might ruin the friendship. The stress of running a podcast of this magnitude has almost done that a handful of times.

We haven't been able to get too much information yet from anyone on the killer. There haven't been any major developments as long as we've been living together and definitely not since we started the podcast. He murdered one more family after he took Delilah's from her, then nothing. He just stopped; vanished into thin air. The town of Milan seems to have started to forget about him, but we haven't. The images of her family are burned into both of our brains. She doesn't talk about them very often anymore, which could be a coping mechanism or maybe she's just moving on. I really don't know and try not to bring it up if I can help it.

"If this doesn't pull him out of hiding, I don't know what will," I say.

CHAPTER 2

COOPER COBB - TWO MONTHS LATER

RING! RING! RING!

The phone lines start ringing off the hook almost instantly in the studio. "The studio." It feels so weird to say that still. When we started this show, we were in my basement, recording together on a single microphone. Internet fame changes that. This was the dream, and it still is.

"You're on the Knock Knock Podcast with Cooper Cobb and Delilah Carney," I say as I answer the phone line ringing in.

"Yeah, aren't you worried that someone will come after you if you continue this show?" says the caller.

"Not one bit," I say, "but thanks for the comment."

RING! RING! RING!

The phone line rings in again.

"Thanks for calling the Knock Knock Podcast. You're on with Cooper and Delilah." I answer a little differently this time, trying to keep it fresh.

"Bro," The caller says, drawing out the 'o' sound.

"Love the show man."

Delilah and I share a look.

"Thanks man, we appreciate it. What you got for us?" I question.

"Oh shit man, nothing. I just wanted to tell you how much I loved the show."

CLICK.

I kill the call. We don't have time for that. Once a week we do a live show and allow our listeners to call in. We usually have a good ten-thousand people listening to us when we do this. Someone has to know something, and some have. We've compiled some decent evidence since we started going live two months ago, just not enough to really make any moves. We have, however, shared some of it on the pre-recorded episodes we upload once a week.

"The fuck?" Delilah mouths to me. I silently laugh. We get those calls weekly. It's annoying because it's not what we are looking for. However, it's nice to hear people are loving everything. Some, of course, are not so happy about the change in the show's format, but you can't please everyone.

It's become my dream, rather, my obsession to solve this case. I eat, sleep, and breathe the Knock Knock Killer. Delilah, too, though not nearly as much. We spend so much time together reviewing evidence, past and present, that some days we forget to eat. Our lives are entirely about the killer. About a year ago, the show became so popular, we were able to quit our day jobs. The podcast pays all of our bills now.

Neither Delilah nor myself are married so when the time came that we were able to quit, we decided to move in together, platonically of course. We're basically brother and sister, though we did make a promise that if we weren't married by the time we are forty, we would go down to the courthouse and just marry each other.

"Alright, the next caller will be the last for this evening," I say into the microphone, letting our listeners know we will be signing off for the night.

RING.

I answer on the first ring this time, eager to shut down for the night.

"Knock Knock, who's there, it's Cooper and Delilah," I say, shaking my head at my poor attempt at humor. Delilah rolls her eyes, but still stifles a laugh. She will never let me know I am actually funny.

The line is silent.

"H-hello?" I say, "Are you there, listener?"

Finally, something comes through the receiver: Breathing. Heavy breathing is all we can hear. I shoot a confused look at Delilah and she gives me the same look back. I listen intently, hoping to catch something coming through. I reach over and turn up the volume on my headphones, but the line is still eerily silent, though I shake it off thinking maybe it's an internet issue.

Maybe it's static, I think to myself. My face is showing a look of perplexity. I'm about to hit the end call button on my computer when another sound that isn't breathing comes through.

KNOCK. KNOCK.

The line disconnects.

CHAPTER 3

DELILAH CARNEY

Grief is a funny thing. For some people, it means sitting in bed crying non stop and asking God what you did to deserve such a thing to happen to you. For others, it's an opportunity to do better, to be a better person in life. However a person grieves, if it works for them, then it works for them. But for me, I'm the latter.

I lost my parents and sister three and a half years ago and for a while, I blamed myself. I blamed myself for many things; for not being there, for not being a better child, for not being present when it all went down. I went through that part of grief, but one day, I woke up and decided to use my sadness and anger as an opportunity to do better and to be better.

Once the smoke cleared and my eyes were open again, I used my emotions to fuel my anger and hatred for the man that took everything from me. The Knock Knock Killer fills my mind most days, but I don't let the thought of the mystery man knock me down anymore. He's not worth that much of my time, though he is worth some of it.

If I ever come face to face with him, I'll kill him with my bare hands. I will make him feel what I felt when I came home that night and found my parents and sister murdered, almost unrecognizable. The cops won't help and haven't for a long time. It's in my hands now. It's just Cooper and me hunting down a ghost.

Cooper loves me; I know he does and that's why he loses more sleep than I do most nights, researching and studying the killer. Although I don't tell him, I think he's bitten off more than he can chew. He has no leads and he has barely any evidence to support any of his wild theories, but I let him rant and rave.

It was his choice to change the podcast and I let him have it. I know he supports me and even though I never considered using our platform to hunt down the person responsible for taking my family, I know they were Cooper's family too. We've been friends for a long time and my family acted as though he was one of their own kids, they really did.

God, I miss them.

I don't think we will ever find the person responsible for taking so many lives, but Cooper is determined to figure out the mystery. Six families were killed by his hand and mine was one of them. Unlike the local police, the city refuses to forget the havoc wreaked by him. About a year ago, the city approached me and the families of the others that were killed. They asked us permission to exhume the bodies of the dead and move them in our local cemetery to a particular spot dedicated to all of his victims. It was a nice gesture and I obliged with their request.

I was there when the reverse funeral took place. I watched as the excavator dug into the ground and when the crane pulled their caskets out of the ground. It was an odd feeling; I thought I'd feel sad watching them be dug back up, but it was the opposite. It was like I had a second chance at closure and it was nice.

Whenever I think about it, the anger that I feel bubbles up like hot magma shooting from a volcano, but I can't let it get to me; I won't let it take me over. If it does, he wins and we can't let that happen. There's no way in hell we will let that happen.

We will find him.

We will kill him.

Grief—it's a funny thing.

CHAPTER 4

COOPER COBB

It had to be a prank call. It just had to be. When you start to get the sort of internet fame that we have, people come out of the woodwork: the fans, the haters and especially with the content we put out, the pranksters. There is no way that could be real. If it were, we are in deep shit.

All I can hear in my head is the knocking ringing in my mind. I try to will it away, but it keeps repeating over and over again. It wasn't even words. It wasn't someone speaking. It was a sound effect. We use them on the podcast all the time but this was different. This wasn't me editing it in. It was a live call.

I stare at the steam wafting out of the top of my lidless coffee cup and I am enchanted by it. I zone into it and keep thinking about the heavy breathing, the knocking. The fact that it was made even creepier when the person didn't speak.

Fans, we can handle fans, even the crazy ones. It just didn't feel like this was a crazed fan. Anxiety is looming in the back of my mind telling me the call was real, not a prank. Even if it wasn't real my mind is convincing me otherwise. Out of nowhere I'm pulled from my stupor.

"What are you thinking about?" Delilah says as she sits down at the table across from me, danish and coffee in hand.

"I think you know," I reply, barely looking up.

She stares at me while shoveling the danish into her mouth and taking a sip of coffee. She swallows then says, "Why are you obsessing?" Her expression is no less joyful than it always is.

Obsessing. I know my obsession with the killer can get a little unhealthy at times, but god damn, Delilah, this was weird. I continue to stare at her as if I'm trying to shoot lasers out of my eyes and burn her.

"You're kidding right?" I say. She laughs.

"No," she says, muffled by the danish stuffed in her mouth. "It was just some weird ass trying to scare us."

Maybe she's right. Maybe it was. My brain just won't let me believe that. At the front of my mind, I want to. I want to believe it and move on and plan for the next episode. Plan for the next recording and the next live episode.

"There is no way the Knock Knock Killer is listening to our podcast." She says, trying to comfort me.

The thought that a serial killer was listening to our show is a little ridiculous, but if I were a serial killer who'd never been caught, I'd sure want to know what people were saying about me, too. I pick up my coffee and take a sip.

"Okay but what if–" I start to say, but she cuts me off. I hate when she does that. She always has to get the final word in and I know she can see the annoyance in my expression and she silently responds with nothing but a sarcastic smile.

"What if, nothing. You're being stupid." She stuffs the last bite of danish in her mouth. I do envy Delilah. I envy her carelessness, I envy her optimism and I envy her ability to not worry so much. It made me think if we ever did try this as a relationship, it might work. Opposites attract right

"Can you just hear me out?" I say, a slight edge to my voice.

She puts her hand to her chin like the statue of "The Thinker," mocking me, pretending to consider my request.

"Hmm. No." She smiles at me then arrogantly takes a sip from her coffee.

I shut my mouth and just sip my coffee as we sit in silence because I know she doesn't want to hear it, she thinks my obsession is getting the best of me. She thinks the call will consume my every waking thought from here on out, but the truth is, we do this show to uncover the truth, to solve the case. Sometimes I think I take it a little more seriously than she does, but I know she wants the same thing I do.

"It was a prank call," she says, breaking the long awkward silence, "nothing more nothing less." Her words hang in the air and the tone she said it with really doesn't convince me one bit that she even believes what she's saying.

"Was it?" I question her while I scan the coffee shop. I'm examining the people around us in the restaurant. If someone knows we are getting close to the truth, chances are, they're watching us right now. It could be anyone here, anyone walking by on the street. It could be any of our friends or family. We are close and someone doesn't want us to be.

CHAPTER 5
COOPER COBB

I sit in my office, poring over the stacks of evidence we have gathered on the Knock Knock Killer, attempting to find any clue who this is. It's pointless, but I have to stay strong for our audience. They're so invested in our show and are looking for answers along with us, even the ones outside of the United States.

The piles and piles of documents we have should have pointed us in the right direction by now, but alas, there is nothing. The killer is clever. He or she—is calculative. They make a plan, and they execute it, no pun intended. The crime scenes show that by the evidence left behind, which is nothing. Well, almost nothing.

At one of the murder locations, the police found a single strand of hair and ran it through the database against all five of the victims, but it didn't match. So they moved on and sent it out to be tested against a broader spectrum of DNA and still received no matches. It was one of the only instances where the killer made an error. The person, whoever they are, must not have a previous record.

The sixth family was the most heartbreaking, aside from Delilah's, in my opinion. It was a mother, a father, a nine-year-old son, and six-month-old twins: one boy and one girl. It was the first time the killer had gone after a family with kids that young. We may never know why they felt the need to kill the babies. I hope we solve this and can find out why.

I sit back in my office chair and close my eyes, thinking. Attempting to make sense of what we do have, which isn't much, but the one question that swirls in my head is: How do they leave nothing behind?

Even the most successful serial killers in America fucked up eventually. Bundy. Dahmer. Gacy. At some point, they all messed up and got caught. Thankfully they did. Please don't confuse my words with sympathy for them. They all deserved to be caught and so does the Knock Knock Killer.

Another suspicion I've had for a little bit is that the killer is not acting alone. Someone has to have a partner to accomplish these sorts of killings. Although that would make hiding DNA a much more hefty job, I can't see how one human being could pull all of this off, especially in this part of the country where everyone and their mother owns a gun. You'd think someone would have been able to fight back at some point, but no one has.

What should the topic of our next episode be? I've never shared the theory that the killer isn't acting alone on the podcast, and I consider that it might be interesting to share. It's a baseless theory, though. I have no evidence supporting it, but audiences like that sort of thing. They like conspiracy theories. They want entertainment that makes them think. Yes, that's the topic.

Through the walls of the living room, I can hear the television blaring as Delilah sits with a bottle of wine, watching her favorite horror movie: Scream. I think about the plot of the film and the climax when Sidney discovers who the killers are: Billy Loomis and Stu Macher.

See? Even Billy had help from Stu. I laugh, thinking about Matthew Lillard's line: "My mom and dad are gonna be so mad at me."

I hear the Ghostface voice through the wall talking on the phone to his next victim. "What's your favorite scary movie?" he says, his catchphrase when he taunts the helpless victim over the phone right before he walks in to slice and dice them.

The Knock Knock Killer has to have a partner, I think to myself. This is a problem, though, because now not only are we trying to solve who the killer himself is, the one who has made a name for himself. We are also trying to figure out who the partner is if there is one. I'm hoping I'm not making a mistake in bringing up my theory.

CHAPTER 6

COOPER COBB

The intro music plays as I announce: "Welcome to the Knock Knock Podcast, I'm your host, Cooper Cobb.

"And I'm Delilah Carney," Delilah says with a slight edge to her voice.

I know she's on edge tonight because I told her this episode's topic would be a secret. I want a genuine reaction from her on record when I announce it. She knows me too well; she knows I only do this when it's something big, or at least something significant to me, and she knows it's outlandish, which, I'll admit it, might be this time around.

Good thing this isn't live so we can cut out any awkward silences and lines we end up saying that we don't want to be included in the final cut, so we don't worry about it.

"So," Delilah says, drawing out the 'o' sound, "...are we gonna do this or not?" A smile starts curving at the edges of her mouth. She can feel it. She can feel the tension between us, making her uncomfortable; I can tell because she doesn't know what's coming, and she wants me to come out with it.

"On this week's episode of the Knock Knock Podcast, a conspiracy theory," I say.

I shoot a look toward Delilah, and the awkward smile begins to fade from her face and is replaced with a slight look of terror.

"Oh boy," she says into the microphone with sincere annoyance.

"Does the Knock Knock Killer have an accomplice?" I ask.

Her eyes widen, and the space around us fills with even more uneasy silence. She looks visibly uncomfortable. She seems suspicious to me.

No, I think to myself, *She's just caught off guard.*

The thought that my best friend could be the accomplice fills my mind, but I shake it off and stare at her, smiling wide. Then she finally breaks the tension.

"Are you trying to get us killed?" She says.

Ah, that's why she looks so uncomfortable. I hadn't considered that before I opened my mouth. I hadn't considered the thought that the killer could be listening, and after the phone call we got on our live show the other night, he might be.

"Listen, Delilah. I'm saying that there is no way one person could pull off all these murders. Think about it. How many gun owners are in our area? You're telling me he just so happens to hit houses where he knows the people won't fight back?" I say, staring into her soul.

"You've said it before, but I'll reiterate; he's calculated, deliberate, and all of the murders are premeditated," she says with a look of seriousness, one I've never seen before. "You think he doesn't know what he's doing?"

"Or her," I chime in.

Delilah looks taken aback because not once on the show or otherwise have I ever alluded to the fact that a female could also be involved until now. She chuckles, then into the microphone, quotes Scream, "The fact is, it takes a man to do something like that."

Without missing a beat, I continue the conversation from the movie: "Or a man's mentality."

She looks surprised again due to the simple fact that I don't watch those types of movies. I don't enjoy slasher films like she does. I'm a crime junkie through and through, but she can't believe I just quoted a line from her favorite movie, and her cheeks turn a light shade of pink.

"Damn," she says, "You do pay attention, I guess."

We share a friendly laugh and continue to discuss the possibility of the Knock Knock Killer having an accomplice, which makes for an exciting and highly entertaining episode. Even though she doesn't agree with me, she carries on the conversation as if she does, challenging me at almost every step but sometimes agreeing. With how often she will admit I might be right, one might think we are married.

As we wrap up the episode, I close the show by saying, "This has been the Knock Knock Podcast with Cooper Cobb." Delilah finishes it by saying, "And Delilah Carney."

"Catch us later this evening on our next live episode at 9 p.m. Eastern Standard Time," I say as I close the show, then cut the recording.

"Okay, you may have some solid points, but I still think he's acting alone for the most part."

I open my mouth to respond, though she knows what I'm going to say and finishes my sentence for me.

"Or her," She says, squinting and smiling at me mockingly. "That was a good episode. I think it's going to help pull in some new listeners."

Suddenly my phone rings, and I dig it out of my pocket and take a look. The screen reads "Unknown Caller." I look at Delilah and show her the screen. She tells me it's probably someone calling about my car's extended warranty, and I should answer it and tell them to screw themselves.

"Hello?" I say hesitantly. There is no sound on the other end of the phone. Just silence, a deafening silence. Then just as I'm about to pull the phone from my ear and hang up, a voice comes across on the other side. "Knock, knock.," the person says with a sinister edge to their voice, then the line disconnects.

I quickly check the software on the computer to ensure we didn't accidentally go live. Nope, just a recorded episode.

I stand there and stare at my phone, Delilah, and back to my phone. I'm confused, but not too confused. We are poking the bear, and it's only a matter of time before it attacks.

"What?" she says, but I can't find the courage to speak.

Someone knows, and someone is pissed.

The problem with uploading content to the internet is everyone has access to it—even the Knock Knock Killer.

CHAPTER 7
COOPER COBB

I lie awake in my bed, staring at the ceiling as I hope sleep will take me away. The dark envelopes my room as I gaze at the ceiling, and I try to close my eyes a few times, but when I do that, I start to envision what I think the Knock Knock Killer might look like.

I imagine the killer in their early fifties with a scraggly gray beard and sunken eyes, similar to Charles Manson, but not quite. I open my eyes to make the visions disappear; of course, that's not conducive to a good night of rest. I look over and tap the screen on my iPhone. 3:35 a.m. Luckily, I make my own schedule, and there is no frustration looming over my head over the thought of having to get up in only a couple of hours to make it to work.

I grab the phone and scroll through Facebook. Maybe I can scroll and scroll and scroll until the boring posts that consume my feed send me into dreamland.

No such luck. 4:45 a.m. Dammit.

I decide to head to my office. If I'm awake, I might as well be productive.

I look over the files, searching for a clue that might help me, and I just so happen to grab one particular photo I'd scanned a million times before. I click feverishly onto the computer and try to Google the image I have sitting in front of me.

It was a photo of one other piece of evidence that the police discovered: a single shoe print found in the mud after a heavy rain outside of one of the victim's houses. The police guessed it was from a combat boot, though no particular brand was ever identified, and the killer wore a size thirteen.

"That's it!" I jump up and yell, then listen intently to hear any signs of movement coming from Delilah's room. The scream was louder than I intended, but I hear nothing. For a moment, I turn around and stare at my screen again, realizing this puts us one step closer. Why hadn't I thought about this before?

I run out of the room, not caring that I would wake up Delilah. I get to her door and grab the handle, then pause for a moment, debating whether this could wait or if I need to tell her now since it wasn't a huge revelation.

Screw it, I think as I swing the door open and barge in like a member of a SWAT team.

"Delilah," I yell as I shake her body to ensure she wakes up fully.

"What?" she says sleepily, her eyes are still not entirely open. "What do you want?"

"It's a man," I say, utterly confident in my findings.

"Oh, nice," she says, uncaring, as she falls back asleep.

She starts snoring again, and I'm not entirely positive she woke up for the encounter. I decide to leave and tell her again in the morning when she is self aware.

I get back to the office and have a sense of pride about myself over what I found. I notice a little green light at the top of my computer screen when I enter the room. It's the light that turns on when the webcam is activated. I slowly make my way to the computer and as I'm right up on it, my eyeball almost touching the camera, the light turns off.

As I slump back down in my chair, my phone chimes so loud that I jump, and I stare at it for a moment, examining the time. 5:26 a.m. Who could be texting me this early? I pick up the phone and unlock it. The message on the screen pops up in the notifications center. The number isn't one I have saved in my phone, and the unknown number pops up as all zeros. A single-word text sends chills up my spine:

Stop.

CHAPTER 8
COOPER COBB

I sit in the Coffee Station in a corner by myself. No coffee, no food, nothing in front of me. Just a getaway. My leg is bouncing off the ground uncontrollably while the anxiety is taking over. I sit and try cracking my fingers repeatedly, even though I know no more air bubbles are trapped in my knuckles. A barista walks up and says, "Sir, can I get you anything?" I just about jumped out of my skin, not expecting her. I look up at her, and I can tell my face probably looks white as a ghost.

"I'm okay," I say, though I'm not.

"Are you sure?" She continues, pressing the issue, "on the house, erm, on me." She smiles at me.

I crack a forced smile at her, and little does she know I appreciate her at this moment more than she knows. I take a look at her name tag, and it reads Tatum. My smile becomes more genuine as she looks at me, perplexed. I look up and catch her eye, and the smile fades slightly.

"Sorry," I say, "my best friend's favorite movie is Scream. Your name is Tatum. It's amusing." I know she can sense the embarrassment on my face.

She chuckles at me, puts a hand on my shoulder, and says, "It's okay; surprisingly, I get that quite frequently." We stare into one another's eyes for a moment, and I see that she's cute, brunette, and has blue eyes. I shake it off when she says, "So how about that coffee?" Still smiling.

"Medium black," I say, "thank you."

"Be right back." She says as she removes her hand from my shoulder and walks away. I wish she would have stayed with me forever, though I'm not sure why. Her touch was lovely, and it calmed me slightly, along with the tone of her voice. She's soft spoken, and her manner is reassuring.

I take a peek at my phone. 9:03 a.m. Where the fuck are you? I think. I called my other best friend, Riley. We've known each other almost as long as Delilah and I have, but he doesn't have an interest in the same things we do and thinks the change to the podcast format was a wrong move. He believes we will dig ourselves a hole we can't climb out of, but he's also much more paranoid than we are, to the point that he has distanced himself from us since the change. He is always there when I need him though.

"Here you go," Tatum says as she returns with my coffee. She sets it on the table and then stands there, making me suspicious, though everything does these days.

"What did you do to it?" I say as a smile cracks on the corners of my mouth, "are you going to watch me drink it?"

She laughs then says, "No, I'm about to go on my break, though, and I was wondering…." She pauses and probably thinks asking isn't appropriate, but she does it anyway. "Do you mind if I join you?"

I think about it for a moment. I can't see any issue, but she can by the look on her face. If her boss questions it, we could say we are friends. I'm willing to help her save face in that way since she's been so lovely.

"I'm waiting for a friend, but it looks like he's going to be late, so, sure." I say, "I'd like that."

She walks away, and I turn the cup around and see the name written on the cup. It's not my name, not even close. The name "Casey" is scribbled across the cup, but I take the lid off and stare.

She returns and sits in the seat across from me, and we sit in silence until I decide to break it and say, "Casey? My name isn't Casey, it's—"   She cuts me off and says, "It was a joke. I know your name is Cooper."

It never stops coming as a surprise when people know who I am. I'm still not used to internet fame.

"Casey Cooper…" she says, "You know, like from Scream," she smiles at me as she looks away slightly.

"Oh," I say with a light chuckle coming through. "Clever," I smile at her, not having the heart to tell her that's actually from Scream 2.

She's cute and funny. I like that. I can't remember the last time I just sat and chatted with another woman that wasn't Delilah, and it's nice to have a fresh face to look at. Don't get me wrong, I love Delilah, but this is different. I have to figure out a way to make conversation. I'm out of practice on this part.

"So, where's your partner in crime?" She says, looking around as if she is expecting Delilah to show up any minute.

"Oh, she's at home sleeping." I say, "So, you listen to the show?" I continue, making conversation about the one thing I know.

"Oh, I listen," she says, pulling out her phone and showing me it's her top-listened-to show on Apple Podcasts, "religiously."

"Nice," a genuine smile flashes across my face, "do you want an autograph?"

She laughs a deep belly laugh and can't seem to stop. Did I go too far? Was that cocky? Did that come off as too arrogant? I didn't mean it that way. It was more sarcastic than anything else.

"No," she says, "You looked like something was bothering you, so I thought if I could take fifteen minutes to try to make you feel better, it's the least I can do."

It's working, I think, almost forgetting why I was even there to begin with; then I glance at my phone again. 9:11 a.m. Where the fuck are you, Riley?

"Well, thank you," I reply, "I appreciate that."

"How's the show going? Do you have any new leads?"

"No," I say, remembering the truth and thinking if I told her, it might scare her away.

"Do you think you will solve it?"

"I hope so. Every serial killer makes a mistake somewhere. We have to wait for him to make a mistake," I say.

"Him? How do you know it's a man?" She questions, holding a snide smile and looking over at me as she sips her drink.

"New episodes are uploaded every Friday at 9:00 a.m.," I say, now sipping my coffee.

"Ooh," she says.

"Oh, yeah," I say, taking another sip.

She looks at her watch, and I feel it's time for her to get back to work. As if she read my mind, she starts to get up and says, "Well, time for me to get back to work. Call me sometime." She places a napkin in front of me with her phone number written on it.

"I will," I say.

As if they planned it, as Tatum gets up from the table, Riley runs into the coffee shop, looking like he just ran a 5K in under fifteen minutes. He's red in the face, panting as though he can't catch his breath, and sweating profusely. He gets to the table and takes a seat. I look at my phone, and without making eye contact with him, I say, "You're late."

"Dude," he says, still out of breath, "I…got…here…as…fast… as…I…could." He takes a deep breath, trying to slow down, then says, "What's the emergency?"

I pull out my phone, which now feels like more of a burden than it usually is, and I pull up the text message from whom I believe to be the killer and show it to him.

"Stop?" he says with a look of confusion on his face. "That's what you made me come down here for? A text that says 'stop'?" His face, which had just started to turn from red to light pink, now turned a shade of red again as his anger gets the best of him.

"That's not all," I say as if I'm trying to leave him on a cliffhanger, "I think I'm being watched…through my webcam."

Riley looks at me and I can tell he wants to argue with me.

"You're full of shit," he says.

"I'm not," I start, "I think I've made a discovery."

"I told you the show was a bad idea, dude."

"I can't stop now. I figured out it's a guy that's responsible."

"How?" he says, the anger on his face now turned to bewilderment again.

"The shoe they found. It's a men's size thirteen; I just used deductive reasoning. I don't know any women with feet that big."

Riley bursts into uncontrollable laughter that causes both staff and patrons in the coffee shop to stare at us. It's an uncomfortable feeling and forces me to slump down into my chair. I turn around to see if Tatum is paying attention, and I catch her gaze, and she lets out a little giggle. That isn't very comfortable, I think.

"Are you kidding me? A shoe? That was your big revelation?" He says, condescension coming through in his tone.

I look down and play with my coffee cup, swirling the liquid inside and not making eye contact. It sounds ridiculous. A shoe print, a single shoe print. That's what I have to go off of, yet at the same time, it's a massive step in the right direction. Assuming fifty percent of the population is female, that's fifty percent fewer people to worry about.

The air around us feels like it's thickening, as I can almost feel the heat coming off of him; irritated that I made him get out of bed for this, then he finally chimes in and says,

"Listen, Coop. I love you, and you're like a brother to me, but this obsession," he starts, "needs to stop."

"I can't do that," I say, "this is my livelihood."

Riley sighs, then gets up to leave.

"That text was a warning, Coop. Leave it alone," he says as he turns on his heels and leaves me sitting at the table by myself again. I turn around and look over to see if Tatum is paying any attention to the exchange, and luckily, she wasn't. I, too, get up to leave, replace the lid on my coffee cup, then walk up to the counter where she is serving another customer. She looks up at me expectantly.

"What are you doing tonight?" I ask.

CHAPTER 9

COOPER COBB

I stand silently, looking at myself in the mirror, wondering if I did the wrong thing. It's been quite a while since I took a woman out, and I am worried I will mess things up. I try telling myself we are just going to dinner as friends, and it's not a big deal, but the anxiety is rising in the back of my mind, and my stomach feels nauseous.

I fix my hair, brush my teeth, then fix my hair again, though it doesn't need fixing, and go downstairs and head to the car. As I walk up to my Chevy Silverado, something doesn't feel right, and an awful feeling rises in my stomach. Delilah stands at the front door like a proud parent sending her kid to the bus for the first time, "Don't do anything I wouldn't do," she shouts at me. That doesn't limit me too much.

I walk up to my truck and notice something odd. It is leaning over towards the passenger side just enough for me to catch, and luckily, it's off-putting enough to force me to check it out. After all, I'm going to have Tatum riding in it with me, I want to be prepared and make an excellent first impression.

I walk around the truck's bed and notice the tire is flat. Not too bad, but just enough to be concerned, and I walk up to check it.

"What the actual hell?" I yell, and I must have yelled loud enough because, through the windows, I can see Delilah running over. I had no clue she was even still standing in the doorway.

"What?" she says before reaching me, "what's wrong?" As she comes around the corner of the front end of the truck, she gasps audibly and puts her hands over her mouth as I stand there, dumbfounded.

I bend down to inspect it: a knife stuck into my truck's front passenger side tire. It looks newer and has a black handle with a silver stripe at each end with a blade at least ten inches long. It's stuck in approximately halfway.

I jump up and look around thoroughly, expecting to find someone watching us as we make the discovery, but we can't see anyone. Just a couple of people walking their dogs; however, the Knock Knock Killer could be anyone, and they could look like ordinary people.

I look back down at the tire and silence fills the air around us. I crouch down and examine the knife, grab the handle and tug hard on it to get it to dislodge from the rubber. It slides out forcefully and I'm knocked back by my own strength. Delilah gasps, probably thinking I was going to stab myself.

"It's a Buck knife.," I say as I continue to inspect the blade's features, "I'm almost positive. I can't tell what model, though."

"So…" She says, "a warning in the form of a text and a slashed tire."

"Yep," I say, just as baffled as she is.

"You've figured out one small detail," she continues.

"Yep," I say as if that's the only word in my vocabulary.

"What happens when we get closer?" She asks, the words echoing in my ear.

I don't want to know, I think, but on the outside, I say confidently, "I guess we will find out."

I can see the fear on Delilah's face, and it's genuine. I know she wants me to stop, but I don't think we can. I know she wants to end the show, but we can't. I know she's scared, but we must be brave right now.

CHAPTER 10
COOPER COBB

I get into Delilah's bright pink Volkswagen Beetle and head over to Tatum's house to pick her up for our date. I am thoroughly embarrassed by the vehicle I'm driving, but it beats the hell out of having to cancel the first date I've had in quite awhile. I reach down and adjust the seat over and over again, but I can't find a comfortable position to sit in so I give up on it. This thing is so damn uncomfortable, I think, the irritation in my mind is increasing every second.

I'm probably just on edge because of the knife that was stuck in my tire and the fact that now we are going to have to drive two hours to Detroit in Delilah's stupid little car instead of the truck. Better fuel economy, but very emasculating and very uncomfortable.

The podcast company that sponsors us and pays for our studio time and advertising thinks with the rise in popularity that our show has had, it would be a good idea for us to do a live show. They want to kick it off at the Fox Theatre in Detroit, which is where they are based out of.

Dee-troit, I say in my head, drawing out the 'e' sound. I'm not thrilled about going there. I wish they'd have kicked it off right here in Ohio; I feel safer here, even with an unknown serial killer on the loose. With everything I've heard about Detroit, Milan, Ohio feels like paradise. Though, maybe it's not as bad as the news makes it sound. They have a tendency to exaggerate the small details for more views.

Speaking of embellishing, that is one thing I promised myself when we started the show—that I wouldn't overstate the facts and I will present them as they are. We act like ourselves, unlike some other podcasters who are there to be actors and actresses and make more for entertainment. The content we cover is our entertainment and it has worked out thus far.

The live show in Detroit kicks off this Saturday at 7 p.m., and I am somewhat excited for it. It's an interesting concept to have a podcast go completely live in front of an audience. It'll be nice to get out of here for a little bit away from the murders, away from the murderer, and away from the small town. Though, as I pull up to Tatum's house, a nagging feeling grabs me in the back of my mind that something is going to follow us. Something evil will follow us to Detroit. I try to shake it off as I see her running out of her house and toward the car. The bad feeling escapes my brain; just her presence makes me forget our current predicament.

CHAPTER 11
COOPER COBB

Tatum gets in the car and slams the door shut, laughing uncontrollably. I don't know her that well, so I don't know why she is laughing at me, though I do have a feeling. It's the pink car, I know it. She's never seen my truck so she probably thinks this is my vehicle–how embarrassing. I glance over at her while we drive to the restaurant, and she's still laughing and smiling, silently now.

"It's not my car," I say, "It's Delilah's."

"It's fine," she says, "pink is my favorite color."

I'm debating whether I should tell her about the truck. Would that scare her away? This is why I don't usually date; I know the consequences that could occur if someone is with me. If the Knock Knock Killer comes after me, they could also come after those that I care about. Delilah, Tatum, Riley, or my parents, even. I decide what to do.

"I walked outside to come pick you up and I had a flat tire," I say, though hoping she doesn't ask too many questions.

"That sucks," she says, "did you run over a nail or something?"

There it is, the question I didn't want her to ask. Do I start this relationship off on a bad foot and lie to her or do I tell her the truth? The debate rages on in my head, then, as if I wasn't debating it, I blurt it out, "Someone slashed my tire."

"Oh shit," she says, chuckling, "who did you piss off?"

"The Knock Knock Killer."

Her chuckling turns to dead silence and I can feel her stare piercing through the side of my head like the knife that I had just pulled from the tire. I immediately regret letting the words out of my mouth and fully expect her to ask me to turn around and take her back home. Instead, she just sits in silence as I continue to drive. I'll take that as a sign that she's willing to take her chances.

"The Knock Knock Killer, huh?" She asks after a long silence.

"Yep," I say awkwardly. "Should I turn around and take you home now?" I ask, dreading the answer.

"No," she says, "I'm not worried about it."

She looks down at her phone and begins texting someone; she's probably telling one of her friends where she is and who she is with just in case something goes down at dinner. I know I would do the same, so I can't blame her at all. What scares me the most about all of this, the warnings, the threats, is that the killer knows where I live now, so, what's to stop him from knowing even more about my life? He knows about Delilah, he probably knows about Tatum, hell, he probably even knows about Riley, even though he doesn't come around much.

We pull into a parking spot downtown in front of the Park Lounge, Tatum's request. I've noticed this girl is simple, she's easy; but not in that sense, or maybe she is and I just don't know it yet. She doesn't want a guy to go over the top, and she doesn't want to be wined and dined; she prefers a simple dinner at a local pub and I'm all for that. Not because I don't want to spend the money on her, but because that would normally be my first choice, too.

She turns to look at me as I reach for the door handle and grabs my hand. She looks deep into my eyes for a moment as though we've been in love for years. She squeezes my hand and smiles.

"It's okay," she says, "you're worth the risk."

She gives me a genuine smile and her bright blue eyes tell me that yes, it is okay. I can feel it in her body language and I can see it on her face that she's being genuine. Even though it's our first date, my heart tells me that she's also worth the risk.

CHAPTER 12

COOPER COBB

The date went over as well as I hoped it would. We laughed so hard we cried and Tatum made friends with everyone in the pub. She is extremely personable and it makes me feel like I made the right choice asking her out. She had the whole restaurant in stitches laughing, though I don't know how outgoing she would be without the couple of Long Island iced teas she had indulged in with dinner. I imagine she's probably just the same considering our first encounter at the coffee shop.

We pull up to her house and enjoy the last of one another's company for the evening. She doesn't look like she wants to leave me and I can't blame her—I don't want her to leave either. Tonight has been perfect and I never want it to end; I didn't think about the killer once. Shit, I think as the mystery person comes back to the forefront of my mind.

I think she notices my facial expression shift from happiness to befuddlement, anger, and extreme focus because she turns toward me and grabs my hands again. She stares me in the eyes, attempting to get me to put my attention on her instead of everything else that's going on around me.

"Look at me," she says, "the two of us are all that matters right now."

Yes. She noticed. She gives me a shy, playful smile and I give her one back. I grip her hands and stare back into her eyes. We enjoy one another for a few minutes and then she takes her arms and wraps them around my neck over the center console, pulling me in close and resting my forehead on hers. She backs off, then closes her eyes, purses her lips, and slowly leans back in toward me.

She stops, then asks while looking up at me with those beautiful eyes of hers, "Is this okay?" I only nod; I yearn for intimacy with another human being for once in my life. It's been a while since I've been in a relationship, and a good relationship at that. Sure, I've had my fair share of girlfriends over the years, but none I ever felt this much chemistry with.

She leans in close to me again, looking for a kiss. Number one rule: when you kiss someone, and you're looking for a nice, long, passionate kiss, close your damn eyes. As I lean in to meet my lips to hers, I open my eyes and look into the short distance to her front yard. I see a dark figure standing there, only illuminated by the light on her front porch. I jump as the sight takes me off guard and Tatum looks at me like she's offended that I opted not to complete the kiss.

I keep staring into her yard, too stunned to speak; I open my mouth, but no sound comes out. I see the figure run off to my right at the same time that I point for Tatum to turn around and see what I am seeing. She turns around then looks at me again with confusion on her face. I'm still pointing out in the yard and she turns around and looks a few more times, making sure she isn't missing anything.

"Good night, Cooper," she says, as she opens the car door and gets out, slamming it.

I sit and watch as she walks up the sidewalk to her front door to make sure she gets in alright. Once she is inside, I get out of the vehicle and look in the direction that the dark figure ran towards and scan the area. I can't see anything at all. I can see some trees on my left rustling, but I chalk it up to the light breeze moving through the residential neighborhood. The only other thing I can hear are dogs barking in the distance. I get back in the car, click my seatbelt, and look in the rearview, checking one more time before I leave.

There's no mistake, I think, *that was the killer, and he's keeping tabs on me.*

CHAPTER 13

COOPER COBB

So, here I lie again, staring at the ceiling, unable to sleep. I know we can't stop. We are close to something, but what that something is, I don't know. Every single minute detail is essential. This guy has been on the run for so long, killing six families, twenty-three people. The images of their lifeless bodies flash in my head and they consume me. It is an obsession, and I can admit to that, but it's an obsession I want and need.

I want to do what the police haven't managed to do yet. The useless, useless local police, the county sheriff, the state police, and the FBI, they all let the case go cold. I understand it to a point, but they barely tried, and it's been some time since he struck another family. Though the threats I've been getting make it feel like something is right around the corner. It feels like I might be onto something. Maybe it is something, and maybe it's nothing. One thing is for sure, though: we can't give up when we are close enough to make him feel the pressure.

If we give up, he wins.

If he wins, more families die.

Not on my watch.

CHAPTER 14

COOPER COBB

This morning, the texts, calls, and emails come pouring in from all over the country. The newest episode in which I dropped the bombshell discovery is a massive hit. Most of the contact has been people saying how much they love the episode. It's the most feedback we have ever gotten from an episode before and I can't believe it.

My phone is ringing and chiming off the hook, and even though it has become almost unbearable, this is the reaction I was going for. By the afternoon, our Instagram and TikTok accounts have hit over a million followers each, and the episode has been shared across social media almost 200,000 times. People want to hear the story, and people want to know and be involved in the capture of the Knock Knock Killer.

This is precisely what we need. Almost two and a half million people across the United States are keeping their eyes out for this person. Though he only killed locally, he could be anywhere hiding, watching, and waiting. Wait, I think, No. He's here somewhere. He's still local. I saw him.

The anxiety I felt the other night comes back more overwhelmingly this time, but it may feel that way because of the adrenaline running through my veins. I can't wait to go live this evening, and I'm going to tell Delilah to be ready for anything. She doesn't know what is happening online because she can't access the accounts—she doesn't want to be bothered with it.

Our accounts skyrocketed even further by 1:00 p.m., only four hours after the hour-long episode went live. We see a huge uptick and almost 1.7 million followers by that point. The interest is there, and the support is confirmed. It's taken us two years to get here. Now that the moment is finally here, it's time to get some factual information, some hard objective evidence, and I am ready for anything.

I run out to the living room and find Delilah watching the news. I come up to her with a giant smile and excitement in my voice.

"Delilah!" I yell, the excitement in my voice uncontainable, "Look at this!"

I sit next to her on the couch and show her our social media accounts and how they have grown in only a few hours. Her excitement doesn't even come close to mimicking mine. She keeps her eyes glued to the television.

"Delilah?" I say. "Why aren't you more excited about this? It's everything we've worked toward."

Her eyes remain glued to the images on the screen.

"We did this," she says, finally speaking up but still making no attempt at eye contact.

I turn and look to see what she's talking about, and the image of a home lined off with police tape and the coroner wheeling out a body on a gurney covered in a white sheet flashes on the screen, then cuts back to the studio.

"Though it can't be confirmed, police say that initial evidence points to this being the work of none other than the Knock Knock Killer," the anchor says.

The banner on the bottom of the screen shows a headline: THREE DEAD IN BRUTAL ATTACK.

I sit and watch the report with my mouth agape as I take in the scene in front of me. Three more dead. Was this because of us? Was this because we started to bring attention to the killer? No, it can't be. Then a photo of myself and Delilah from my personal Facebook pops up on the screen, and my heart sinks.

"Cooper Cobb and Delilah Carney, the pair that run the popular 'Knock Knock Podcast', are already being blamed by local residents for the carnage that took place at the home late last night," She says.

Our mouths drop even further. We are getting blamed for the murders.

"How?" I shout at the TV as if the news anchor can hear me, causing Delilah to jump.

She continues, "Some say local law enforcement should make them shut down their show and stop provoking the killer."

"If we are going to solve this, we need to work around the clock," I say, still staring at the screen.

I fully expect Delilah to fight me, to beg me to shut down the podcast, but she doesn't and instead replies with, "I agree."

A silence falls between us that feels like it could drag out for hours, though it only lasts a couple of seconds; then she breaks it and says, "Let's take this bitch down."

Just then, a rapid, intense knocking hits our front door. We stare at one another for a moment. Both of us are frozen in place, too afraid to see who is there, when we hear, "Milan Police, open up." A sigh of relief falls between us, and we look at each other. Even though it's a relief, I think we both have the same feeling about where this is headed, and then there is another rapid knock at the door.

I get up from the couch and open the door where two Milan police officers are standing. One of them is a more prominent man, probably standing about six foot four, muscular with a mustache that I have to look up at, and a female cop, much shorter than him, with tied-back brown hair.

"How can I help you, officers?" I say, acting like I hadn't just been watching the news.

"Cooper Cobb?" The male officer says, trying to sound intimidating, while the female officer, in a much sweeter tone, says as she looks through the doorway and into the living room, "Delilah Carney?" .

"Yes," we say in unison.

"You're under arrest for the murders of the Roberts family."

CHAPTER 15
COOPER COBB

The cell they put me in is precisely as I expected, similar to how they show it in movies. It's a small, approximately ten-by-ten square with a concrete floor and bars from floor to ceiling. I'm sure prison is much more comfortable than the holding cells at the local police department, but luckily they kept Delilah and me in the same cell. The ground is cold and stone solid, and there is a single bench. They have us packed in like sardines with others who, like us, had been arrested.

I'm sure the others weren't tossed in here for something as extreme as murder, though, and that surprises me when I think about it. I'd think we would be separated from people like the one guy standing in the corner who does not attempt to communicate with us. He is pretty drunk and sways back and forth while another man talks to himself or, possibly, his imaginary friend. I'm not too sure.

Delilah and I look at one another as we wait for them to come to get us. We haven't been given a phone call yet. I already know who I'm going to call, but we have to wait for the detectives to take us out for questioning. Maybe we should have shut it down. Perhaps we should have just stopped while we were ahead. It's getting out of control, but now we are in too deep. We need to keep moving forward, even if it means getting tossed in jail for a brief moment.

"They don't have anything on us," Delilah says, breaking the silence between us.

"I know."

I'm not in the mood to talk to her, but it's not like I'm pissed at her; I am pissed at the situation we got ourselves into. I'm surprised she hadn't already told me what I know we are both thinking about the show. As if she is reading my mind, she says, "We can't shut it down, you know."

"I know," I say, the only words I can get to come into my brain.

What if we had shut it down? What would life look like right now? I wouldn't be doing what I loved, and I know I'd probably still be working my dead-end job at Best Buy. I know that, but those were simpler times and I wish to have that back right now.

"Cobb, Carney," an officer shouts, "come on." He walks up and unlocks the door. I shoot him a dirty look, which is not my intent, it just went across my face, and I try to stop it as it happens, though a little too late as he notices and gives me a look of irritation in return.

We follow the officer out of the holding area and into another room where the walls are stark white and bright LED bulbs shine so bright throughout, it makes me squint as we walk in. The walls are bare, except for one wall that has some mirrored glass on it.

"Sit," he says as he points at the table smack dab in the middle of the room.

He pulls out two pairs of handcuffs as we sit down at the table, wraps them around my wrists, then Delilah's, and secures them to a metal ring in the middle of the table.

"Detective Carpenter and Detective Prescott will be with you in a minute," he says as he walks out of the room.

We sit in silence as we wait out our fate. We could go to prison for life, never solving the case of the Knock Knock Killer. Wow. Is that the biggest thing I am worried about right now? My life would be over, our lives would be over, and everything would be ruined. The door to the interrogation room opens slowly and deliberately, and in walks two male detectives, both very large and intimidating. I unintentionally gulp at the sight of them.

As they sit down in front of us, they keep their eyes locked as if we have a chance to escape, but quickly one of them chimes in, "Hi, Mr. Cobb." Then he looks at Delilah, "Hi, Ms. Carney." We sit in silence, and I nod as Delilah leans back in her chair as far as the handcuffs will let her, trying to distance them.

"I'm Detective Carpenter, and this is my partner, Detective Prescott," he starts. "We want to ask you about the Roberts family murder."

Detective Carpenter sits and stares with a straight face, stern, trying to unnerve us. It doesn't work on me, and I see what's happening here as I notice Detective Prescott sitting with a smile. Good cop, bad cop, I think. We shouldn't answer questions without a lawyer present, but fuck it. We don't have anything to hide. The silence in the room, coupled with the soundproofing of the walls, makes it almost unbearably quiet.

"We don't know anything," shouts Delilah suddenly with a panic-laced scream as she slams her fists down on the table.

I wince as her scream startles me and hangs in the air.

"Woah, woah," says Detective Prescott, holding his hand toward her. "No one in this room is being blamed; we just want to talk."

"Then why did your guys arrest us for suspected murder?" Delilah asks demandingly.

"It's a formality," says Detective Carpenter, "we know what the news is saying, but we don't think you're involved."

The two of us stare at the detectives for a minute with confusion. Why are we being detained, then? Why are we handcuffed to the table? The questions are swirling in my head, and I gesture to the handcuffs and shake my hands, hoping they can take a hint.

"Ah, yes," says Detective Prescott, pulling a key out of his pocket and unlocking my handcuffs, then Delilah's.

We both rub our wrists, then I ask, "So, gentlemen, what do you want to know?"

Detective Carpenter leans back in his chair, looking me in the eyes, and says, "We want to know what you know."

I laugh; detectives are asking a couple of podcast hosts for their input on a serial killer. This whole thing is ridiculous, so I reply with a silly answer, "So, not fans of the show?" The pair stare at us for a moment, astounded by what I just asked. It may have come out a little too sarcastic, though. If they listen, they would know that we don't know much that they don't already know.

"Oh, we've listened to your show," says Detective Carpenter, "and no, we aren't fans, just useless cops."

Yes, they have listened, and I can feel the heat and the redness of embarrassment flash across my face as he recites what I say on the show all the time; that they're just useless cops. Whoops. It may not be an intelligent line to use when we live in such a small town, but our audience is much larger than Milan, Ohio.

"I said what I said," I reply, trying to sound confident and slightly arrogant, "but then, if you've listened, you know everything we know."

Detective Carpenter sighs, and I can tell he hoped we knew more than we've put out in the open, but that is it. I wait for one of them to reply, then I say, "I have a suspicion it's a man based on the size thirteen shoe print that was found and that he may have a partner helping him carry out the murders, but those are my only theories." That's precisely what they are—just theories.

Detective Carpenter looks under the table, then back to me.

"Mr. Cobb, what size shoe do you wear?" He asks accusingly.

"Size eleven, why?" I ask.

He stares at me with a look of suspicion on his face. It feels like he is staring into my soul, but maybe he is trying to get a rise out of me. Maybe he thinks if he stares long enough, I'll break down into a confession—but I won't confess to a crime I didn't commit.

"It's just—" he says, seemingly considering keeping his mouth shut.

"What?"

"I'm going to give you some strictly confidential information. If you share it with anyone, and I mean anyone, I will haul your ass back in here and ensure you will never see the light of day again. Do you understand?"

I can see sweat beading up on his forehead as he says this. A mix of the temperature in the room and nervousness, I'm sure.

"Absolutely," I say, "I won't say a word."

This must be pretty good, I think.

"When we arrived on the scene this morning, we found the Roberts family stripped of their clothing and their bodies lined up in a row in their foyer," he starts.

I stare at him intently waiting for the rest of the story.

"They had," he pauses for a moment, "words—carved into their abdomens."

I look over to Delilah and she looks at me. Her expression is mixed with concern and confusion.

"How does this pertain to us?" I ask.

He opens up the manila folder that's sitting in front of him and pulls out a piece of what looks like photo paper. My guess is that it's a picture from the crime scene and he's about to show us something that's going to shock, and probably disgust us.

"This isn't for the faint of heart, I want you to know," he says, "are either of you squeamish?"

Both Delilah and I shake our heads. He flips the photo around and my hands instinctively shoot up and cover my mouth in surprise and disgust and Delilah gasps. It is a photo from the scene of the crime—a photo of the family, dead, lying in their foyer. We both stare for a few seconds, unable to look away even though we want to. There are words carved into their abdomens just like he had said—not words, rather, names. Our names are sliced into them; mine into the dad, hers into the mom, with their little boy serving as a placeholder for the word 'and.'

"You're telling me this wasn't you two confessing to the crime?" Detective Carpenter asks.

We can't do anything but sit and shake our heads and all I can think is how strange it is for the killer to be leaving a calling card, but the more I think about it, the more I can't believe it is a calling card—maybe it's more of a warning. Another warning for us to stop pursuing him. He's going to come after us and we need to be ready for anything he throws our way.

For a moment, I consider sharing with them the threats I'd been receiving, like texts, phone calls, and even the slashed tire. They already know about one threat, the carvings on the bodies, but I decide it's best not to share with them. They'd ask us to shut things down immediately or issue a cease and desist order. Delilah must have noticed what I'm pondering because she reaches over, grabs my arm, and squeezes to warn me to keep my trap shut.

"So, are we free to go?" I say. "I'm sorry we can't help you with anything else."

The two stare at us, then Detective Carpenter reaches into his pocket and pulls out a business card.

"Sure," he says, "but if you hear anything, let me know." He hands me the card, and I stuff it in my pocket. We all get up and head toward the door, and, like the gentleman I am, I let Delilah through first; then, as I walk away behind her, Detective Carpenter says, "Mr. Cobb?" I turn around and look back at the tower of a man.

"I'd consider shutting down the podcast if I were you," he says. I don't think he meant for it to come out the way it did, but it sounded like a threat to me. I turn back around and look at Delilah, who is slightly shaking her head no.

"I'll consider shutting it down when you produce a cease and desist letter," I say, then I turn around and walk away without another word to him. I'm not going to let the detectives pressure me into something I don't want to do, at least not until it's legal. For now, we push forward.

CHAPTER 16
COOPER COBB

Delilah and I brace ourselves as I prepare to hit the button for us to go live. If the live show has a response like the pre-recorded one did, we are in for an exciting evening. But if the live show goes anything like the rest of the day, this will be a shitshow.

"You ready?" I say to Delilah, and I can see panic hitting her facial expression as she takes a deep breath.

"Let's do this," she says.

I hit the button, and the listeners start rolling in as I begin the intro music and the announcement, "Welcome everyone to another live episode of the Knock Knock Podcast…." I begin, pretending everything is alright. I have to pretend everything is okay; chances are, I don't even have to mention our quick jaunt to jail. Someone is bound to call in and ask us about it.

We start with our usual conversation, just like we always do, with a quick recap of our week, how we are doing outside of the podcast, and what's been going on in our lives. I watch the listener count as it increases.

One thousand.

Four thousand.

Eleven thousand.

Twenty-two thousand.

The phone lines have already begun to ring off the hook, and we aren't even there yet. Messages coming through in the live chat read the usual things we see every week.

I love you guys.

Your show is the best.

One message stands out to me and sends chills up my spine. Delilah feels the same thing I do as she reads the message on her laptop and looks up at me.

I have information about the killer. Answer the phone.

I tell our listeners, "We are going to take a quick break to hear a word from our sponsors." I don't want to raise any alarms, and this is the best way to have a quick private conversation with Delilah. I take us off the air and start running the ad reel.

"Did you see that message that just came through?" I say to her excitedly.

"I can't keep up tonight; they're coming and going so fast," she says, "but I caught that one."

"Should we just start taking calls early?"

"Let's do it."

I wait for the last advertisement to end and make sure to mute the audio on that track then put us back on the air. "And we are back," I announce, "since everyone is so excited to get through, we are going to start taking calls early tonight."

The phone lines start ringing like crazy, and I have to grab a line and run through it quickly. Unfortunately, we can't get to everyone, so I want to ensure I get to talk with the person who sent the message. I take multiple calls from different people just wanting to call in and say "hi," say "hi" back, and quickly cut the line to take the next call.

"If you're the one that sent the message about having information," I say, "please call in; we are waiting for you."

I have to think of something as the calls continue, but the person that sent the message wasn't calling in again. I don't want to call them out in front of 56,000 people who are now listening, but I have to do something.

65,000 listeners.

68,000 listeners.

The list continues to grow, and it's officially our most successful and most listened-to episode yet. The feeling is exciting but terrifying simultaneously, and I glance up at Delilah, who is feeling the same way.

RING! RING! RING!

I grab the line and answer, "You're on with Cooper and Delilah."

"Yeah, I sent a message to you guys," the caller says as I breathe a sigh of relief. The other end of the line stays silent for a moment, and a message appears in the live chat again.

Can you voice disguise me?

"Absolutely," I say into the microphone as I flip the switch for the disguising function which brings a caller's voice way down in pitch, hiding their true identity.

"Okay, you're disguised, caller," I say.

"So, I live in your area," he proceeds, "and I was out driving around last night."

I can tell he is nervous by how often he pauses in his speech and the shakiness I can detect in his voice.

"I drove by the Roberts home last night, and there was some movement that caught my eye," he says.

Delilah and I look at one another and hang on bated breath. Was he going to tell me exactly what I hoped he would say?

"Two figures dressed in all black with black hoods covering their faces were slinking around the house, so I parked my car and turned it off," he continues.

"I watched them break down the door and enter the house. I immediately heard gunshots, so I picked up my phone and dialed the police."

My jaw falls to the floor as I listen to this shocking new information, but I'm also baffled because I was right. I knew it wasn't just one person. I knew he wasn't working alone. I had called it.

"I heard the sirens in the distance, and by the time that happened, the two figures were running out of the house," he finishes.

"Wow," I say, "thank you for your call."

I am almost too shocked to speak, but I must carry on. I have to keep him on the phone. I have to ask more questions.

"Did you get a good look at them?" I ask.

"Decent."

"Any idea on height, weight, anything like that?"

"I could tell one was a man. He was tall, probably over six feet, and from what I could make out in the darkness, he was fairly muscular. The other one was shorter, possibly female by the walk, but that's all I could gather," he confirms.

I can't find the words for a response, so I say, "Thank you so much for your call. This changes everything."

Without saying another word, the caller disconnects the line. Delilah and I sit in silence for a few moments while the phone lines continue to ring off the hook. We have confirmation. A male and a female teamed up to take down as many families as possible. My theory panned out, but that raises a bigger question: Why?

CHAPTER 17
COOPER COBB

"…I watched them break down the door…."

The caller's words are ringing in my ears. The Knock Knock Killer is not and has never been known for breaking and entering. Is this even the original killer, or is this a copycat? There was always a quick rap of two knocks followed by waiting for the homeowner to come to answer. Always. It's getting worse, and it's time to pick up the investigation. The local police won't help. They may have reopened the case, but that doesn't mean they will be any closer to solving it than they were the last time.

Why were our names carved into their stomachs? I know what it is, but I don't want to admit it. It's a warning. It's a warning for Delilah and me to stop. It's a warning that we could be next, but I can't stop. I won't. We need to solve this thing and put an end to the killer.

I'm sitting at my computer going over everything we already have. A shoe print, a single hair with no DNA match, the names carved into the victim's bellies, and then it occurs to me and I can't believe I haven't thought of it before. Can we figure out what kind of knife was used? Can we compare it to the other victim's injuries to confirm he uses the same knife every time?

Some news outlets, the more shameless ones, actually got their hands on the crime scene photo from this morning. They've been showing it all day, and it's been popping up all over social media despite the police's efforts to pull it from the platforms. Admittedly, I saw it and saved it to my files. I couldn't let it go missing.

I open the file containing all the crime scene photos and examine the stab wounds against the carvings. All of the injuries do look like they came from a similar blade. It helps me determine that based on the reasonably large knife collection that I have myself.

As I pore over website upon website attempting to identify the blade, there's a knock on my office door. I don't think much of it and say, "Come in." Delilah walks in and sits in the other rolling office chair in the corner.

"You okay?" she says, knowing my mind is running a mile a minute.

"I'm fine," I say, attempting to convince her I am, "just trying to identify the blade that caused the injuries."

"You've got to stop obsessing," she says. I roll my eyes, but with my back turned, she doesn't see it.

"I'm not obsessing. I'm researching," I say.

"It's unhealthy," she says, completely ignoring me.

We sit in silence for a moment. I don't want to argue right now. I'm focused on the task at hand, and she wants to fight me right now. Sometimes it feels like we are married. We bicker like an old married couple, but that happens when you've known and lived with someone as long as I've known and lived with her.

I continue to stare at the screen, and out of nowhere, my phone begins to vibrate. I try to ignore it until the call gets sent to voicemail. The vibrating stops and I glance over, but return my gaze to the screen almost immediately. I can't be distracted right now. I feel like I'm getting close, and then, it dawns on me. I'm looking at the stab wounds of the first family that the killer struck.

"Holy shit," I say.

Delilah sits up straight but observes me as I run around the room, gathering up all the knives in my collection, not saying a word. I must look manic, like I finally lost my mind over this. She's going to have me institutionalized. I throw my stockpile on the ground in front of her, and she jumps out of the way as if the blades will jump out of their cases and stab her by themselves.

"Watch it," she yells.

I continue to sift through the pile while saying "no" out loud as I examine each knife and set it to the side repeatedly until I find my Buck 119 knife. I hold it up in front of my face, and Delilah looks concerned, leaning further back in her chair as though I'm going to stab her. I examine the blade and take it back to my computer, then pull the knife out of my drawer that was stuck in my tire that I had stashed away. I hastily type in the address for the Buck Knives website and pull up the specifications table.

"Point one-seven-five inches thick," I say, quickly clicking back and forth between the crime scene photos and the knife, "one inch in width." I use a digital version of a measuring tape to determine the size of the stab wounds on the victims. It reads one to one and a half inches.

"Could have stabbed and slit," I say to myself aloud. Finally, I look again at the last victims' photos, the ones with our names carved into them. I look at the image, the knives, and my hand. I flip the blade around, so the end is pointed downward, shut my eyes hard, and bite down on my tongue so hard I might bite clean through it.

I place the end of the knife in the palm of my hand and press down and bite even harder. The pain of the blade pushing through my skin is almost unbearable as I drag it down the length of my palm, and the blood starts to run out.

"Cooper, what the fuck?" I hear Delilah scream in the corner of the room. I turn around and glance at her face; a look of sheer horror has taken the place of her normally joyful visage. I look back to my hand and pull the knife away, then hold it up to the photo, zooming in on the words carved into their abdomens.

"We have a match," I say as Delilah runs out of the room, quickly returns with a towel, then presses it to my hand to stop the bleeding. She yells at me again, "Are you insane?" Then, a text flashes on my phone:

Come Over.

CHAPTER 18
COOPER COBB

It's only been five minutes, and the towel is soaking with crimson red. I'm sitting in the bathroom waiting for Delilah to return with gauze to wrap it properly before heading to Tatum's house. As I sit, I think about everything we've been through up to this point and everything we have uncovered about the case. Do I turn over my information to the police? There's nothing solid, but it's more than they have ever figured out.

Delilah enters the room as though she's my savior, shaking the gauze in my face as she strolls in. She has me sit on the vanity while she sits on the toilet, and I remove the towel from my hand. She inspects the cut, using her maternal instinct on me as she debates making me go to the hospital for stitches, and I know what she's about to say.

"It's not that deep," I say before she can comment, "and if I go in, they'll ask me a bunch of questions to ensure I'm in my right mind."

Delilah laughs at me. "Well, we know you're not," she says, "you're fucking insane."

We share a laugh, the first genuine laugh we've shared in weeks. I'd invested myself so deeply in the case and uncovering the truth that I'd forgotten my friends and family. I need to reconnect, and while this may be what I feel to be my purpose in life, I can't keep forgetting about those closest to me. If I get too close to the truth, this could end badly, and I'll need them.

Delilah applies Neosporin to my hand, then looks at me and says, "I'll be right back," leaving me alone in the bathroom as blood seeps out of the wound; luckily, it's not pouring out anymore.

I hear the office door open. She never goes there unless I'm in there, though I don't mind; it's not like I'm hiding anything from her. I sit and listen, and after just a minute, she comes back.

"I needed the medical tape," she says, "why were you keeping medical tape next to the scotch tape on the desk?" I shrug.

"Probably because we never moved in fully," I say.

She laughs, then says, "So organized with all the case files, not with anything else."

"My life is a god damned natural disaster," I reply, though she already knows my organizational skills are garbage.

She finishes wrapping up the laceration on my palm, ties up the gauze, and tapes it for extra support. Delilah has an excellent bedside manner, she'd have made a great nurse, but it's not the life she ever wanted. She has the smarts, the courage, and the personality for it, just not the desire.

"There," she says, slapping the cut, "rub some dirt in it." She smiles at me but continues holding my hand and stares deeply into my eyes. Something in the pit of my stomach starts to flutter, a connection I'd never truly felt before, especially with her. She leans closer slightly as if she's looking for a kiss.

No, I think, I can't.

"Don't do anything you're going to regret," I say to her, and a look of disappointment flashes across her face.

"You're right," she says, "sorry, I just—" I cut her off before she can finish her sentence.

"I know."

Instead of a kiss I know we would both regret, I throw my arms around her and pull her in for a deep, tight embrace. We hold one another for a moment, genuinely enjoying the company of the other, then she breaks the silence.

"I don't want to lose you," she says quietly.

CHAPTER 19
COOPER COBB

As I pull up to Tatum's house, I take a moment to reflect and feel proud of my accomplishments and strides in getting closer to solving the case and bringing the Knock Knock Killer to justice. I need to remember and take these little moments to enjoy what we've done and how far we've made it in this short journey. It's game time, but how do I take everything I know and make some connections?

I consider again, for a fleeting moment, to report my findings to the police. I grab Detective Carpenter's card and stare at it, considering my options. When we met them, I felt like he would be the one to take things a little more seriously; maybe he would finally be the one to solve it with my help. No, I think. They'll take my information, stash it away, and it will lie to die like the rest of the case. I need to do this on my own. I place the card back into my center console. I'm still not sure I won't need his help sometime soon.

I get out of the car and head up the sidewalk to Tatum's front door. The house looks empty, almost deserted. She did tell me to come over, so she has to be here. The motion-sensing light on the front porch turns on as I get closer, and I can see the front door is open slightly—still no lights on in the house either.

I try to look through the crack of the slightly ajar door. There's no movement inside. I push the door open just a bit more to get a better look. I can't hear any activity anywhere in the house.

"Tatum?" I say, but there's no answer. My heart begins to race, and my hands start to shake, thinking the absolute worst has happened to her. Without another minute, I run back to the car and grab the handgun that I stash under the passenger seat. If the killer got to Tatum, there's a chance he's still here. There's a chance I can catch him and end this.

It wouldn't be his normal M.O., but as we've seen recently, there are new rules to his sick and twisted game. That's what makes catching him so difficult. That's what makes identifying him almost impossible.

I run back up to the house clutching my pistol, stopping briefly as I get to the door listening for movement again—still nothing. I push the door open and start darting from corner to corner like a special agent with the FBI, flattening my back to the wall each time I move.

It seems no one is here, not even Tatum. I slowly traverse the stairs and head up. As I get to the top of the stairs, I notice a flickering light underneath a door, and as I inch closer and closer, making my steps lighter as the distance between myself and the room closes in.

I stop at the door and listen, but there's still no sound. I look around the landing and back down the stairs, ensuring no one is there. Nothing. Before going Rambo on the door, I lightly grab the handle and check to see if it's unlocked. It is. Slowly I push the door open and look in.

I can see a nicely made bed and a single flickering candle on the bedside table. The room emanates the scent of lavender vanilla, and I take it in for a moment, reminding myself not to get too distracted. Then I spot it; one corner of the room seems to be out of illumination from the light, and I can see some movement. I hold the pistol up in front of me and inch closer; suddenly, the figure ducks down, and I hear a scream, "Cooper, don't shoot. It's me," Tatum yells.

"Come out slowly, Tatum," I warn. Though I'd fallen head over heels for this girl, I didn't know her that well, and I wouldn't have any qualms about shooting her if she tried anything.

She walks out slowly into the light where I can see her with her hands in the air, a look of genuine fear shoots across her face. She's wearing a bathrobe that's not tied closed, and I can see her wearing some very sexy black lingerie underneath it. On the second date? I think to myself.

She walks out to me and, with her voice shaking, begs, "Please put the gun down." I turn the safety back on, empty the chamber, and place the gun in the waistband of my pants. She hugs me and says, "I'm so sorry I scared you. I was trying to be…." She stops for a moment.

"Trying to be what?" I ask.

Her face turns red with embarrassment as she finishes her statement with, "…sexy." She says, turning even redder, "I guess I'm not that good at this sort of thing, huh?"

I look her up and down, admiring the lingerie she wore for me, and grab her by the waist and stare into her eyes, "No," I say, "bad timing is all."

"My bad."

"So, uh," I say, "what were you planning for tonight?"

She pushes me away and laughs, then looks herself up and down. I'm not stupid; I know what she planned for; I'm just unsure

I want to. For one, it's only our second time together, unless you count that day in the Coffee Station, and for two, I'm not sure I can focus enough on her.

She comes toward me, grabs my waist by the belt loops on my pants, pulls me in real close, and says, "Woah, is that a gun, or are you just happy to see me?" I roll my eyes at the dumb joke, but this girl is worth all the cliches in the world. I grab the gun from my pants and set it on her bedside table.

The world slowly begins to disappear, and it feels like she and I are the only ones that exist. She kisses me, slowly, passionately at first, then the physical frustration takes over, her lips moving much quicker and her tongue reaching inside my mouth.

She takes off my shirt as our primal instincts take over. I unclasp the back of her bra, admiring her half-naked body on top of me, running my hands down her sides and reaching around the back, grabbing her ass. She lets out a half smile as I grind into her pelvis, the flame inside us like an out-of-control wildfire.

She rolls over and slips her underwear down, grabs them from under the blanket, and tosses them to what I assume to be the dirty laundry pile. My eyes follow them as they fly through the air and land on the floor, and I notice something glimmering in the candlelight underneath the mass of clothing. Still, before I can overthink it, she reaches over and grabs my groin, and I turn to find her staring at me with a smile.

The heat, the passion, the unadulterated ferocity between us is almost too much to handle as I slip my underwear down and get on top of her, holding her wrists and restraining her. She seems to like it as she tries to get out of it and touch my body, but I won't let her. She begs for it as I slide inside her, and she lets out an audible gasp and closes her eyes tight.

I continue, though the thought of the shining object under the clothes pile overtakes my mind, and I can't focus on her. She doesn't notice, though, thankfully. Her body language tells me she's close, and I am too.

We finish at the same time, and I flop to the side of her, out of breath.

"That…was…" I say.

"Yes, it was."

We smile at one another, and I turn my head to the side, staring at the shining object under the clothes pile, still unable to turn my attention away from it. She gets up from the bed, puts her robe back on, and goes to the bathroom. This is my chance. I quickly throw my clothes back on and run over to the pile, listening intently for the toilet to flush.

I move the clothes to the side and slide my hand underneath, grabbing a long hard object and feeling around for what it might be. It stabs my finger, and I pull my hand out quickly. It seems like nothing at first, but then a drop of blood begins running down my finger—nothing like the wound on the palm of my hand. I reach underneath and grab the handle. I pull it away from the clothes, and it holds onto one of the articles as I reveal a Buck 119 Special knife hidden away with a pair of black gloves.

I feel like the dumb character in every horror movie when they don't know who the killer is, except the roles are reversed. Usually, it's a female that unknowingly sleeps with the male killer.

I hear the toilet flush, and the sink starts to run. This is my chance. Do I run without saying a word or confront her about my discovery? The sink shuts off, and I'm running out of time. Panic begins to set in. Knife still in hand, I grab my pistol off the side table. My decision has been made as I cock the gun back and chamber another round. I point it up and wait for Tatum to exit the bathroom and back into the bedroom.

The door opens. It's now or never.

"Cooper, what the—" she says.

"No. I will do the talking. What the fuck is this?"

She examines the blade in my right hand as my left-hand shakes, gun pointed right at the girl I, just moments before, had given me the best sex of my life.

"I don't know," she says, crying, "I've never seen that before."

"It was under your clothes," I say as I gesture to the pile of laundry, which is now deconstructed.

"Tell me the truth, Tatum," I scream as she begins to cry even harder.

"Cooper, I swear, that's not mine," she says through her tears, her entire being now shaking from the fear that I'm going to put a bullet between her eyes.

I examine the blade again and notice something I hadn't initially. Where the edge meets the handle, I see a dark red spot crusted to the metal. Blood? Is that fucking blood?

I remain frozen in place, unsure whether to believe her or not. If I think she is and we go on with our lives, and I'm wrong, she could kill again. She could take off, leave, never to be seen again, and continue her reign of terror elsewhere. I stop, take a deep breath and stare her directly in the eyes.

"Tatum, you have one chance and one chance only," I say, threatening her, "Are you the Knock Knock Killer?"

CHAPTER 20

COOPER COBB

My thoughts are racing as I run home to tell Delilah what I've found. I'd fallen for this girl. I'd fallen head over heels. I wouldn't say it was love by any means, not yet at least. Now the chances of falling in love with her are zero. She was perfect, or so I thought. I'm unsure if I should call the police this time, tell them everything I know, and let them handle it. Should I shut down the show? No, I think, I can't do that. I can't shut down now. I've unmasked one of the killers. I've unmasked the accomplice; now, who is the responsible one? Who started this all those years ago?

I pull into the driveway squealing the tires. It must have been louder than I thought it was. I jump out of the car and see the neighbors looking out their windows, trying to figure out where the noise came from. Delilah opens the front door before I can even reach it, and I run inside and right past her.

"What the hell are you doing?" She shouts at me. I'd never heard her so angry. I forgot that I was driving her Volkswagen, not my truck.

"I'm sorry," I say, out of breath, "I-I—"

I have a hard time catching my breath. The sheer panic taking over my entire body makes it difficult to breathe, and I sit down on the couch, taking a moment to compose myself so I can tell her the news. As my breathing slows, she moves to the sofa and sits beside me. She puts her arm around me to comfort and slow me down.

"What's wrong?" She asks.

I pull the blade out of my pocket and throw it down on the floor. She looks down at it, then back to me, then back at the blade, and back to me with a horrified look. She's stunned into silence and seems to want to say something, but can't.

"Tatum…" Still trying to catch my breath, I start to say, "Tatum…is…the…killer."

The statement pushes her to remain silent. I can see she's trying to come up with something, though the words just aren't coming into her brain. She opens her mouth, then closes it multiple times, and finally gets the words out, trying her best to remain calm for me.

"Okay," she says, "start from the beginning. What happened?"

"So, we were having sex.…" I begin.

She jumps back, just as surprised as I am that we did that on only our second date. She stares at me, mouth wide open, then, "You fucked her?"

"C'mon, Dee," I say, "yes, I did. Anyway, that's not important."

"Wait…how was she?" She says with a smile on her face, trying to keep it light.

"Not important," I say. "…I saw something shining under her laundry pile, she went to the bathroom, and I found that," I say as I point to the blade lying on the floor.

I'm still not entirely convinced she is the Knock Knock Killer, but maybe the accomplice. I'm still not convinced that she is responsible. That may be the trick, though. It's always the person you least suspect. Every horror movie I've ever seen makes that abundantly clear.

The air around us feels like it's thickening, making it harder to breathe. As I come down from a panic attack, my heart starts to race again, my palms are sweaty, and the world around me feels like it's starting to spin. Delilah can sense my erratic breathing, and she wraps her arms around me again and pulls me back, making me lean back into the couch and relax. She places the palm of her hand on my chest, breathing deliberately, expecting me to match her pattern.

Slowly but surely, my breathing slows, my heart rate returns to normal, and the sweat on my hands dries up. I open my eyes to see Delilah staring at me; the look on her face is one of love, compassion, and empathy. This girl cares for me, and I'm starting to think I pursued the wrong one, as if finding the knife didn't solidify that already.

"You okay, Cee?" She asks, still smiling at me.

"Yeah," I say as I return the smile to her, "I'm okay now."

She stares into my eyes for a moment with her arms tightly wrapped around me. She tousles my hair a little bit, like a child who just got done crying, and runs her fingers through it. She leans in and, without hesitation this time, kisses me. Not a friend-type kiss either; a long, hot passionate kiss that sends chills down my spine and flips my stomach upside down.

I reach up and grab her behind her neck, returning the favor. The kiss feels like it's lasting forever, and I don't have a way of describing it, but it feels…right. It feels like the first time my lips have touched another person's lips. After what feels like an eternity, she pulls away and stares into my eyes again, and we take a moment to just enjoy one another.

"Better?" She asks.

"Much."

"So," she says, as she leans back away from me, "what are we going to do about that?" She gestures at the knife lying on the floor. I think for a minute, debating the proper way to go about this. Do I continue to go rogue or report it to the police? The look in her eyes tells me everything I need to know, though getting the police involved in a case they didn't care to solve the first time around is unsettling at best.

I mull it over for another minute, and I can see she's getting antsy as she anticipates my answer. I'm unintentionally keeping her on the edge as every possible scenario plays out in my head. What if I'm wrong? What if she's not to blame? What if she's telling the truth? Do I risk sending an innocent woman to prison for nothing more than a hunch? The physical proof needed to lock her up for life is sitting in front of me, though; what if it was planted in her room? The question continues to ring in my head.

What if?

CHAPTER 21
COOPER COBB

I woke up this morning to sounds of pounding, one in my head and the other at the front door. I grab my head as the migraine slams around, making my head throb, my eyes hurt, and my stomach turn. I get out of bed and go to my bedroom door and open it. At the same time, Delilah opens her bedroom door. We look at one another, wondering who could be visiting us right now.

I grab my head again and signal Delilah to answer the door. She understands. I run to the bathroom, grab some Ibuprofen, and toss it into my mouth, swallowing hard as the pills slide down my throat. I look at myself in the mirror. I almost don't even recognize myself. The unkempt hair, the scruff sticking out of my follicles, the dark circles around my eyes, this isn't me; this is the image of a man who has had it with life. I'm going to have to do something with how I look before we head to Michigan tonight.

I walk out of the bathroom and head to the front door to see what all the knocking is about, and as I round the corner into the living room, I see Delilah standing there with Detective Carpenter and Detective Prescott. Why are they in my living room? What happened now?

"What did I do this time?" I ask with obvious impatience and frustration in my voice.

"Mr. Cobb," Detective Carpenter says, "we received a tip this morning that you may be in possession of the murder weapon." I quickly glance at Delilah, and she shakes her head. She's the only one that knows I have it, and now I have to think on my toes. Do I lie to them, or do I hand it over?

"Please," I say, "have a seat." I gesture to the kitchen, and the four of us walk in and sit at the dining table.

"Coffee?"

I'm trying to bide my time while I come up with an excuse or give myself up. I walk over to the cupboard, grab the coffee and filters out, and begin filling the coffee maker.

"Please," says Carpenter, "black, two sugars."

As I put together the coffee, it becomes abundantly clear that the detectives, while they agreed to stay for coffee, are becoming impatient with me not answering their questions.

Think, Cobb, think, I say inside my own head, then, without turning around and looking at them, I say, "Who told you guys I have the murder weapon?" Though I know they'll not give up their source, the question buys me some more time.

"Anonymous tip," says Prescott, finally piping up, "she saw you with a knife."

There it is. She. Tatum must have called them. She must be pissed about my accusations, so she acted the only way someone caught can. She blamed me, hoping I wouldn't be able to report her.

"Hmm. She, huh?" I say, letting them know I caught on to the slip-up.

I turn around and look at Detective Prescott, whose appearance is usually one of joy, now showing a dejected look on his face. He knew he slipped up and hoped I hadn't caught it, but I did. The details aren't lost on me these days. It's my job to know all the details. I pour the coffee, drop two sugar cubes into the mug, and hand it over to Detective Carpenter; all the while, Delilah is tracking my every move. Even she can't figure out where I'm going with this.

I sit at the table with my own mug of black coffee and stare at the three as they stare back at me. The Detectives attempt to read my body language and Delilah stares at me questioningly. None of them say a word.

"So, if I were to hand this 'murder weapon' over to you," I say with air quotes around "murder weapon."

The three of them wait on bated breath.

"Will you listen to me?"

Carpenter and Prescott look at one another as though they are making a silent agreement. They look back at me and say, "yes," in unison.

I nod my head. Delilah looks horrified, and I can read her mind. All my hard work, all our hard work. Everything we have discovered is about to get turned over to the police, more than likely for all of it to go into a file and never be opened again. The good thing is, I have copies, and if they think I'm going to stop my investigation, they're so wrong. I won't stop until the Knock Knock Killer is in cuffs or underground.

CHAPTER 22

COOPER COBB

It's a surreal experience to see your own name in lights. We pull up to the Fox Theatre in Detroit, Michigan, where so many different artists and incredibly famous bands have played shows. The marquee on the building reads: The Knock Knock Podcast w/ Cooper Cobb & Delilah Carney. It's amazing and the two of us both stare in awe. This is show business. We've made it.

I can tell that crossing the border from Ohio into Michigan lifted some weight off of both of our shoulders, though I am still carrying the weight of last night's events. I'm still trying to wrap my brain around the fact that I potentially slept with the killer, or, at the very least, the killer's accomplice.

We arrived here much earlier than anticipated and earlier than we needed to. Neither one of us has ever visited Detroit, again, mostly because of all the negative things the news tells you, but it's actually a beautiful, bustling city, especially at the heart of it. We visit a place that the locals call "Greektown," and I can imagine it's called that because of the casino that sits right in that area.

There are many different things going on right now, possibly because it's a Saturday night. There are a lot of bars and nightclubs open and we watch as drunk people stroll and stumble down the sidewalk, proudly wearing Detroit Lions gear. There isn't much I can say about sports, but one thing is for sure, even in Ohio, we know the Lions aren't a great team. Michiganders stand by them though.

The sun is starting to go down and the downtown area is lit by the massive amounts of lighting coming off the buildings here. There isn't a sign the night life will be slowing down any time soon.

We finish off our dinner at Pegasus Taverna, a Greek restaurant inside of the casino, and wait for the bill. We are sitting in a booth by the window and can see out onto the street. I glance at my phone and see the time, 5:05 p.m. Luckily everything in Detroit is walking distance, so it's only about a fifteen-minute walk to the theater and we don't have to be there until six, giving us plenty of time to get there.

Delilah must have noticed, too, because as our waitress walks by, she catches her attention and asks her to bring us two shots of Jameson. I give her an annoyed look, and she just smiles then says, "You look tense, you'll thank me later."

The waitress returns with the two shots and a copy of the bill in her hand.

"Will that be all for you two this evening?" She asks.

"Maybe two more sh—" Delilah starts until I cut her off.

"That'll be all, thanks," I say, with a smile.

The waitress walks away, and Delilah holds her shot glass up over the middle of the table. "To a great night and a great show," she says, and I hold my glass up and we clink them.

I down the shot, shake off the liquor face, and wipe my mouth. I glance out the window and in the remaining sunlight, across the street, I can see a person dressed in all black with a hood over their face. I stare for a moment, then shake the thought off, literally shaking my head while closing my eyes. There's no way he followed us, I think, and when I open my eyes, he is gone. I look around frantically and notice the waitress is at the table next to us. I interrupt her taking their orders.

"We'll take two more shots of Jameson, please."

CHAPTER 23
COOPER COBB

"Ten minutes to showtime, you two," a stagehand says, peeking into our dressing room. This is it; this is the moment we've waited for; this is our big break. We already live the dream that every podcaster imagines when they upload their first episode but being on stage in front of a bunch of strangers that actually paid to come see you in person—man, that's a rush.

I look over at Delilah and she looks back at me. We smile at one another and take it all in. Everything here has been catered to us; they even did our hair and makeup for the big event. That's lucky for me because in the chaos of everything that happened this morning, I totally forgot to do anything with my unshaved beard.

Delilah runs over and gives me a huge hug and big, wet kiss on the cheek as the clock ticks down until we have to be on stage. The plan is this: topic discussion, crack a few jokes, talk directly to the crowd, then a Q&A session with the audience. That Q&A session scares me, though. We are used to it on the Friday night live shows, but in person, it's something totally different.

"You ready, Cee?" Delilah asks me.

"As ready as I'm going to be," I reply.

She grabs my hands and pulls away quickly then says, "Oh yeah, you're nervous," as she wipes the sweat from my hands onto her pants. I am nervous, very nervous. Not so much about the show, but more so about what I saw at dinner. I didn't tell Delilah. She's in too good of a mood and I didn't want to ruin it for her. The stagehand peeks his head in again and calls us to the stage with a five minute warning. We walk out of the dressing room, checking our hair one last time in the mirror on the way out.

We get backstage and we can hear the crowd getting rowdy. I peek around the curtain to get a good look at what we are dealing with. The place is packed, and I can't see a single empty seat. Anxiety swells in my body and I feel like I'm going to be sick. I can see sound guys, assistants, and more running around like crazy backstage. All these people were hired by the distribution company strictly for us and for tonight. I stop a stage production assistant and he runs by us and caught off guard by my hand suddenly on his arm, he yells and jumps.

"Sorry, but, how many people can this place hold?" I ask.

"Just over five thousand," he says, "every last seat sold out tonight."

Every single seat in the house is sold out. People who want to see us live and in person. I can't believe it. I look over to Delilah who I don't think really grasped the gravity of this event until now, either, as her mouth is hanging open, surprised by what the production assistant just told me.

"Wow," she says, "five thousand seats and every single one is sold out."

"Yep," I say, reverting to my limited vocabulary.

Both of us peek out the curtain this time and look out into the crowd. People of all ages are finding their seats as the announcer on the loudspeaker kindly requests them to sit and ensure their phones are off or on silent for the show; "We will begin in one minute," he says.

"Wow," Delilah says again, evidently losing her ability to find another word as well.

"Yep," I say in response.

We pull the curtains back and look at one another. This is the last time for the next two hours that we will be able to be ourselves. I grab her by the waist and pull her in tight to my body and she throws her arms around my neck. Without hesitation, we both lean in and kiss. Right then the production manager walks up to us and says, "Sorry to interrupt, but fifteen seconds."

We pull back and walk to our starting point before walking out on stage. The production manager follows and mouths "five, four, three, two, one," all while also counting down on his fingers. He points at us to tell us it's go time and we walk out on stage. The crowd goes insane and the stage lighting shining down on us is so bright. I squint as we walk to our seats, waving to the crowd, though we can barely see anyone.

The crowd begins to settle down and we sit down on the sofa, which is quite comfortable. It's not like the hard fold-out chairs that the studio provides and what we are used to. I imagine I'm sitting on the set of Late Night With Jimmy Fallon enjoying that level of comfort. With microphones in hand, I say my now somewhat famous opening line.

"Welcome," I say, dragging it out a little more than I do when we record, "to the Knock Knock Podcast; I'm Cooper Cobb,"

"And I'm Delilah Carney," Delilah says. We smile at one another, then toward the crowd.

***

The show went as well as it could; we had the crowd laughing, we had them engaged, and we had them eager to ask us questions. We take a short intermission then head back to the stage for the Q&A session. All in all, the actual show portion lasted about an hour and a half, which means we have about an hour left for questions. As we walk back out to the stage, I remember the mystery person I saw across the street from the restaurant and the hairs on the back of my neck stand up.

We sit back down on the couch and I attempt to keep my composure, but Delilah shoots me a look and I know she knows that something is wrong. We have to keep up appearances though, so I take a deep breath and raise the microphone to my mouth. As I open it to speak, Delilah cuts in.

"Alright, everyone, are we ready for that Q&A?" She says, looking my way reassuringly.

The crowd goes wild; people are cheering, screaming, and have their hands shooting up in the air. The production assistants make their way to aisles where they will stand with microphones at the ready when we call on someone. I look out to the crowd and can actually see how many people are there now. During the break, we requested the lighting crew to turn the lights down for us. As I look out at the faces staring back at me, I feel nothing but pride for this show and what it's become.

"Fire away," Delilah says.

It seems like everyone's hands shoot up into the air at the same time and the assistants are standing at the ready for us to point and call on someone. Some people are pushing their hand up toward the sky, attempting to make it look like their question is more urgent than everyone else's. Delilah calls on someone in the second row.

"You, in the red shirt, second row," she says, while an assistant runs over and hands him a microphone.

"Thank you," he says, "have you two ever considered when you come up with more extensive evidence, the killer might come after you?"

We hadn't mentioned any of the warnings we'd received from him already; we didn't want to bring it up to the fans. Not yet, at least. Delilah looks at me and I look back. Almost telepathically, in that moment, we decided together that we would give him the answer he's looking for.

"He already has," I say. Some in the crowd gasp as the words come out of my mouth.

"Yes," I continue, "in the last few days, I've received several warnings from the killer directly."

I stand up and pace the stage as though I am a stand-up comedian. I throw a hand in one of my pockets to give the illusion that I am laid back about it.

"If you were listening to last week's live episode, you'd have heard him call in on two different occasions," I continue as some of the people in the crowd drop their mouths wide open in surprise.

"He's also sent me a couple of text messages, slashed the tire on my truck, and has shown himself to me twice," I pause for dramatic effect, "always in the dark, always covered head-to-toe in black and wearing a hood."

The crowd remains silent as I reveal that the killer has shown himself to me. They look petrified.

"Who's next?" I ask. A ton of hands shoot up in the air and I point about ten rows back, right in the center of the auditorium.

"You, in the blue hat," I say, as another production assistant runs up to him with a microphone.

"Piggybacking off the last question," he starts, "what's your plan then, since you guys don't have a clue who this person is?"

I think for a moment. If the killer is here. If he is here in Detroit, watching us, I want him to know we are serious and I want him to know that this isn't for show; that we will take him down. I look back at Delilah and she gives me a nod of approval, knowing what I'm about to say. I don't need her permission, but it's nice to know we are on the same page.

"We will find him," I say, "and when we do, we will kill him."

The crowd fills the auditorium with thunderous applause and cheers. I feel proud of that answer and I wave Delilah up to join me at the front of the stage. For a moment, we stand and enjoy the spotlight, literally and figuratively. As people are beginning to sit back down, just barely, I can see a figure all the way in the back row with his hand raised. I can't make out a face, but it seems he wants to ask a question.

"Yes, you, all the way in the back dressed in black," I say.

The production assistant hands him a microphone and the crowd falls silent awaiting his question. The room is so quiet you could hear a pin drop in it; the quietest it's been since we started a couple of hours ago. A few people turn their heads to get a look at the person holding the microphone.

"What's your question, sir?" Delilah asks.

A deeper, gruff, almost threatening voice comes through the speaker system as he begins to speak, slowly and deliberately.

"Hello, Cooper and Delilah," he says, "Knock, Knock."

My eyes widen and the man throws the microphone and runs out the emergency exit to our left. As the microphone hits the floor, feedback pops through the audio system causing many in the crowd to throw their hands over their ears. I look at Delilah and do the same as him, throwing my microphone and jumping off the stage.

I run up the aisle and toward the exit and as I frantically push the door open, I'm out in a back alley. I look left, then right then left again. There is no one around.

"Come and get me, you pansy-ass motherfucker," I yell, seemingly at nothing.

PART 2

CHAPTER 24
TOM LANGFORD

I picked up a hitchhiker last night. He seemed surprised that I'd pick up a stranger. He asked, "Thanks, but why would you pick me up? How do you know I'm not a serial killer?" I told him the chances of two serial killers in the same car would be astronomical.

If you asked me why I kill, I don't think I could give you a straight answer. It may be the feeling of freedom it gives you. It could be the powerful energy you exhume, especially when no one can track you down.

I couldn't tell you why I killed a living thing for the first time, but it wasn't a human. The first living being I ever murdered was a frog with a **BB** gun, and even that gives you a rush nothing can match. Some people enjoy roller coasters to give them adrenaline, and some go base jumping or skydiving. I kill. It's euphoric. It's therapeutic.

Along with that, I think it's vengeance. My soul yearns for revenge, and that's something no one can take from me. Not the police, not the FBI. No one. I kill families and strictly whole families. I take them all down one by one. I don't chase lone teenagers through dark alleys and murder them, and I don't target children; that's fucked up, by the way.

No. I kill the entire family. I don't discriminate whether it's mom, dad, sister, brother, aunt, or uncle. Whoever is there at the time gets taken down.

It's probably my past that did this to me. I was abandoned and left to my own devices at a young age. My dad left, and my mom left. When I was seven years old, I was left behind with nothing but the clothes on my back.

Seven years meant nothing to them. Just like that, I was left at the fire station. For the next eleven years of my life, I was thrown around from foster home to foster home until I was old enough to be on my own, then once again, I was thrown out into the cold, cruel world to fend for myself. I'd already been on my own, so I knew I could handle it, but I found a different way to pass the time.

My first massacre took place at the age of twenty one. I found myself drunkenly walking home from the bar on Christmas Eve, stumbling all over the place, and that's when I spotted them. I looked up to see a family through their windows enjoying one another. In my stupor, I walked right up to the door, knocked twice, and as soon as the dad answered the door, I pulled out my knife and stabbed him right in the guts.

STAB.

STAB.

STAB.

Three times. I watched as the blood poured from his stomach and the rush of killing that frog returned. I hadn't felt so happy in a long time, so I pushed the old man over and ran into the house, killing the mom and the two kids.

Up to this point, I've repeated the process five more times. But I decided to stop three years ago. I thought my luck would run out and I'd be caught eventually if I kept going. I took three years to plan, scheme, and figure out how to continue getting away with it.

Three years ago, the local police in Milan, Ohio, gave up along with The FBI. They named the case of the Knock Knock Killer a cold case and quit searching for me, but now there's a problem:

Cooper Cobb and Delilah Carney.

CHAPTER 25
TOM LANGFORD

Cooper and Delilah, the hosts of the Knock Knock Podcast. They're my most recent problem. For three years, I've lived a life of solitude, of peace. Then, ironically, these two came knocking on my doorstep. They devote their lives to finding me, tracking me down, and solving the case. I've made it my mission to make sure they don't.

Tonight they're live on their show. I listen every week, but they don't know it. Tonight I want to scare the absolute shit out of them. I want to send a warning. I want to entice them to stop digging, to stop looking, or else. I listen as they take a few calls. Usually, they're just bullshit calls. "I love the show," or, "I love you guys so much." Those types of calls.

I hear someone say, "Yeah, aren't you worried that someone will come after you if you continue this show?" Cooper, naturally, says he's not concerned. He can't look weak to his callers. I laugh. The thought that this child could take down a notorious serial killer is amusing.

"Fuck you," I say out loud, "Fuck you, Cooper Cobb."

He should be worried. He should be terrified. Him and Delilah. I'll kill them both. I'll tie them to a tree and slit their eyelids open so they can't look away while I gut the other one. They won't find me, and the two of them will become another number in the list of those I've maimed.

Hmm, I think, Delilah could be useful to me though.

I pick up my phone and dial the number listed on their podcast show notes. This is the first of many warnings I'll send to them. I listen as the phone rings, though I don't expect an answer. I'll give them credit, they do have a lot of listeners. It's inspiring—not to me, but I'm sure to someone.

"Knock, Knock, who's there? It's Cooper and Delilah," I suddenly hear on the other end of the phone. I didn't plan well for this. I didn't think they were going to answer. I sit for a moment in silence, though I'm sure my raspy, nervous breathing could be heard on their end. I take the phone from my ear, and distantly I hear, "H-hello?" I'm taken aback, "Are you there, listener?" I panic. I don't know what to do, so I put the phone on speaker and place it next to the side table next to me, then knock on the table twice before hanging up the phone.

I smile proudly, but I know it will take a little more to scare this little prick away.

CHAPTER 26
TOM LANGFORD

I think the phone call unnerved Cooper. Yes, it had to. It wasn't much, but it was something. I have to do anything I can to get him to stop using his platform to find me. If he finds me, it's game over. If I don't make him stop using his show to hunt me down, then I guess as a last resort I would go against my typical motive and kill him.

Kill Cooper Cobb, I think, *sweet, sweet justice.*

Cooper doesn't know that I've run into him in public a few times. I've seen him with my own two eyes. I've seen him at the grocery store, I've seen him at the local coffee shop, and one time, he slipped up.

I was drinking my caramel macchiato at the Milan Coffee Station, enjoying the morning when Cooper walked in. He's a tall, pretty boy and slightly muscular, but no match for me. I could have easily followed him into an alley, taken him down, and that would have been the end, but no. I'm playing the long game. He thinks he's tracking down a ghost, but I've been right here the whole time.

Watching.

Waiting.

So I observed him as he sat in the coffee shop alone. He must have gotten up to go to the bathroom because one moment, he was there, and the next, he was gone. His black coffee was on the table lidless, the steam wafting in the air, and his phone was next to it. Who leaves their phone? I saw it as my chance.

I got up, left my coffee behind, grabbed his phone, and sifted through the files to see what he had on me. Nothing. Also, who doesn't set a passcode on their phone? Is he that big of an idiot?

Quickly, I set up a tracker on his device. Now I could follow him anytime I wanted. I could watch, wait for my chance to strike, or mess with him a little bit. I wanted to be inside his head, and I wanted to be the only thing he thought of morning, noon, and night.

I set the phone down, returned to my table, and waited for him to return. I pulled up the app on my phone. The tracker was installed successfully. I could see the icon for his phone in the exact location as mine. Now I could get inside his mind. I could show him who he's messing with. I could make him look like he's slowly losing his mind, with hopes that someone institutionalizes him for his delusional thoughts.

Tonight, he's back at the Coffee Station, and he doesn't know it yet, but I am too.

Watching.

Waiting.

CHAPTER 27

TOM LANGFORD

I'm back at the Coffee Station ordering my drink, and a beautiful young girl named Tatum is taking my order. I hand her my cash and look behind me. I see a young man sitting at a table alone until another young girl joins him.

"Excuse me," I say to Tatum. She looks up and meets my eyes, "is that Cooper Cobb over there?" Her eyes light up as she looks me deep in my eyes, then toward Cooper and Delilah's table.

"Yeah, you know him?" She says, "He and that girl with him, Delilah, run a huge podcast."

I observe the pair; Delilah is carelessly shoving a danish into her mouth while Cooper sits with a look of anxiousness on his face. They're talking, and Cooper looks a little intense while Delilah shrugs off whatever he's saying. I turn back and look at Tatum while she hands me my change.

"Are you a fan?" She asks me.

"Yeah," I say, "huge fan of the show."

I shoot her a quick smile and she returns one back to me and make my way to the end of the counter to retrieve my order. I grab my coffee and take a seat. I watch the two closely, but not too closely. I don't want them to catch me staring.

The longer I watch, the more nervous I am that I will be caught. I always need to remind myself that I may know who I am, but that doesn't mean anyone else does. I look over and see Cooper, and suddenly he's scanning the coffee shop with a look on his face that says, "I feel like I'm being watched."

I quickly look down at my phone to make it look like I'm not paying any attention to him and mindlessly scrolling Facebook. When I look back up, they're gone.

CHAPTER 28

TOM LANGFORD

It's not enough for me to scare them a little bit. I want to terrify them; I want to horrify them. I want to cause them pain. I have a terrible feeling that Cooper knows something that the police missed. I don't know what it is, but deep in my stomach, I feel something is off. Something isn't quite right.

I should send another warning. I look at the tracker and the two are in town; I need clarification. I zoom into the map and take a closer look, noting the nearest cross streets, then moving over to my laptop to get a closer look. Hopefully Google Maps has come through and maybe there's a street view uploaded to get the closest look possible.

Pulling up Google Maps, I simply type in Milan, Ohio. It's a small town. The population is approximately 1,400, so it will be easy to zoom in. I find the corner of North Huron and Church streets and click on the little person icon and drag it right onto the main road, cross-referencing with my phone where it's showing me Cooper's current location.

I click and drag the map and spot it: it looks like they're at someone's house. In my observations, they're at this location a lot. They must be recording this week's episode. I think of a plan of action, grab my things, and run out the door. I'm going to meet them there. I'm going to do something. I have to. I need to keep this going.

***

I pull up to what I believe to be the studio and wait for a moment, the darkness enveloping me. It's late at night, and downtown Milan only has a single working streetlight right now. I feel even more powerful in the dark. Like a shadow, I can maneuver without being seen or caught. Though it's the nighttime hours, that doesn't stop the carefree residents from being out.

I observe as a group of college girls from the neighboring city stumble out of the single bar we have in town: Wonder Bar and Grille. They're stumbling all over one another, laughing so hard they're crying. I wish I'd had the opportunity to experience that much joy. I never did. Friends were another thing I never had the chance to have.

I see a woman in a sports bra and yoga pants jog past me with a dog leash attached to her wrist and an Australian Shepherd running about fifteen feet ahead of her. The carefree attitude everyone in this town has pisses me off. I'll show them. I'll make sure no one ever forgets the Knock Knock Killer. I haven't killed in a while, but that's all about to change.

As the girls from the bar fall over one another as they walk past my car, I pull out my phone. I ignore their giggles and their joy. I'll show them. I'll show them all. I dial Cooper's number, which I took down when I placed the tracker. This time I have a plan. I'll make him squirm and I'll get inside his head.

The phone rings a few times, and then he answers the phone with a "H-Hello?" I stay silent for a moment. I don't want to be too quick, so I take a second to build the suspense. I'm theatrical in that way. I thought he might hang up, so without another second, I breathe deeply.

In.

Out.

"Knock, knock," I say. The tone in which I said it surprises even me. It was menacing. It was threatening. It was exactly what I was going for, and then I click the end call button.

CHAPTER 29
TOM LANGFORD

It's early. I can't sleep. The rush of adrenaline I have from that simple phone call is astounding. It's almost on par with killing a human being, but not quite. I'm getting closer to sending a proper warning. An actual sign, but I had to find a target. Admittedly, I'm out of practice. Most of the time, my kills were random, but this next one needed to be perfect.

I scroll through Facebook and Cooper's profile pops up in my People You May Know section. I click on it, scrolling through his feed to get to know him better, but he offers no insight into his personal life as most do on social media. Just a funny meme here and there and links to his podcast littering his page. I glance at the time—5:19 a.m.

Jesus. I need some sleep.

I scroll back to the top of his page, about to exit, when I see the green icon on his profile photo that indicates he's online. What could he be doing this early? Is he, like me, also unable to sleep? Maybe I messed with him enough that his body is physically and mentally on edge and unable to rest. Maybe I've broken him. No. It's too early for that. I want to paralyze him with fear, and I've only just begun.

I jump up and grab my laptop and log in. I've hacked into his computer and I activate the webcam so I can see his every move. I watch as he re-enters the room, then, I see him look right into the lens of the camera and slowly walk toward it. Does he know I'm watching? I quickly log out just in case.

I pull out my burner phone and type his contact into the text message bar. I type a single message, pause for a moment, then hit the send button—one word. I smile, proud of myself as I admire the message. It's not much, but the single syllable could be enough to keep him on edge and keep him at bay.

Stop.

CHAPTER 30
TOM LANGFORD

I'm incredibly proud of myself for the warning I sent to Cooper. I unlock my phone and check to see where he is. The Coffee Station again. Jesus, he drinks a lot of coffee. I sit and ponder what to do next, and I pull the famous Buck 119 Special out of my side table drawer. I say famous because it's the blade I've used for all the murders.

Every. Single. One.

Yet somehow, they've not been able to identify it. I don't leave much, if anything, behind, but that should have been the easiest thing to identify. I don't think the police even tried if I'm being honest.

I head out to the garage and fire up my bench grinder. As it spins, I lightly touch the knife's edge, sharpening it, ensuring it's ready for my next victims. I used a blade duller than I preferred once, and it didn't quite get the job done. It did plenty, don't get me wrong. I won't leave witnesses, but it took extra coercion to make it happen. Aside from Delilah's family, he is the only one of my victims that I vividly remember; his face is an image that's burned into my mind.

The blade didn't make quick work of the act, and he lay dying slowly as he looked up at me. He couldn't see my face, but I could see him. The twisted visage of a dying man is nothing I ever want to see again. Do I feel bad? My conscience isn't that strong, but physically watching someone die instead of just knowing they died —not fun.

I stare at my reflection in the metal as I sharpen the knife. Sunken eyes with slight wrinkles on the corners tell a story of a man who has seen some shit. My stringy beard is out of control. The perfect image of a killer, in my opinion. Forget Gacy, forget Koresh, forget Watts; they may have higher body counts than me, but they were caught much faster. I'd be the poster child if there were a serial killer fan club.

I glance at the phone again and see the indicator start to move. Cooper is on the move, and as I watch it, I see him pull into a driveway, and the phone begins to move inside a house. That must be his home. I pull the blade up in front of my face, examining my work. It looks sharp enough to do some damage. I run my thumb along the sharpened edge, and with a yelp, I pull my hand back quickly. A stream of crimson red droplets run down my hand, and I smile as I look at myself again on the side of the blade.

"Sharp enough," I say aloud.

My phone begins ringing, and the sound makes me almost jump out of my skin. I look at the contact name calling in and smile.

"Hello," I say, in greeting, "I was wondering when you'd call."

The person on the other line has been watching Cooper, too. They are waiting for their chance to take him down. That person is my partner, my help, and the love of my life. If I'm caught, so are they. I listen intently, then say, "So you want back in the game, huh?"

CHAPTER 31
TOM LANGFORD

I pull up to Cooper and Delilah's house at dusk. The sun is barely above the horizon, and darkness quickly consumes our small town. I observe for a moment and see some motion inside through the front window. It's Delilah. There is no sign of Cooper being anywhere near, but his truck is still in the driveway.

I can't waste any time. I pull out a pair of black jersey gloves and slip them over my hands. I wince slightly as the fabric rubs against the fresh laceration on my thumb. It feels like a paper cut. I reach over and grab the knife, observing myself in the blade again, a prideful look on my face. I may have warned him already, but this would be the start of the more extreme warnings.

I take another quick look at the house to ensure I don't get caught, and I swing the car door open and run across the street, quickly hiding behind the Silverado in the driveway. I press myself against the vehicle's bed, panting and out of breath.

In the distance, I spot a police car coming down the road and I quickly flatten myself on the ground, roll underneath the truck, and wait for the vehicle to pass. I spot the brake lines and think I could just cut them and end things now. Nope. I came here to scare the guy, not kill him, not yet.

The car passes, and I quickly pull myself back up and head over to the passenger-side front tire. I grab the knife, stab the tire swiftly, and decide to leave the knife stuck into it. The hiss of the air leaving the tire fills the air around me. I get ready to take off, get in the car and go, and then I hear the sound of the front door opening. I jump up and look through the passenger window. No one is standing in the doorway. This is my chance.

I dash across the street, swing the driver's side door open, and hop in, reclining the seat quickly and flattening myself as much as possible. I can hear some inaudible talking across the street. He must have discovered the tire. I take a few deep breaths, trying to slow my heart rate. I can hear my heart beating in my ears. I hear a vehicle start-up and peek over the window just slightly. The sun is down now and the streets are primarily dark, so I shouldn't be discovered. I see a pink Volkswagen drive past, and the front door is closed.

"That was fucking close," I say out loud, letting out another breath.

CHAPTER 32

TOM LANGFORD

I drive home, proud of my accomplishments over the last twenty-four hours. The sheer panic Cooper feels must be eating at him and wearing down his confidence, drive, and commitment to bringing me down. I'm almost confident that the next episode he uploads will be him admitting defeat and shutting down the podcast; then, I can go back to my life of solitude.

I fantasize about the peaceful life I once had. There was no running from the police or the FBI, and there was no looking over my shoulder everywhere I went. Everything had fallen into place. I had gotten away with my crimes. Crimes. I know they're crimes, and I shouldn't be this proud of getting away with it. Twenty-three murders, and they found nothing but a single strand of hair that matched with nothing.

That was the only slip up I made, and it was relatively unavoidable, not truly my fault. I'd always taken the proper precautions. I take a left on Berlin Street, almost home. This whole time I've only been about three blocks away from Cooper's house. I've passed him on the street a million times, I'm sure, and he has no idea who I am. A smile flashes across my face as that powerful feeling of being invisible comes to mind again.

I'm about to pull into my driveway when I look down the road. I spot the pink Volkswagen Beetle again. What the hell? I think. It's only four houses down, so I sharply pull into my driveway, the brakes grinding to a halt. I get out of the car and stare down the road for a moment, knowing I need to investigate. I still have the gloves on, so I grab a knife and a ski mask, sliding it quickly over my head as I run across the street.

I cut through the few yards that stand between myself and the vehicle. As I enter the yard of the house it is parked in front of, I drop lower to the ground. I can't be spotted now. I've come too far. I strain my eyes, attempting to see the occupants inside the car. That's when I spot him.

Cooper. Fucking. Cobb.

I can't reasonably determine who the second person is in the car. I can see long hair in the passenger seat, but that's about it. I slowly take significant, deliberate steps across the yard so I don't alert them. I can now see into the passenger seat and spot Tatum from the coffee shop. I can't believe my eyes. They look like they're just wrapping up a date.

My eyes dart up to the house, which stands out against the darkness. A single porch light is on in the front. I know what I must do now, but how do I go undetected? I slowly back away from the car, and it doesn't look like they even have a clue that I am there.

I run around the darker side of the home and spot a terrace running the height of the house to the upstairs. The roof looks flat enough to walk on carefully. I start to climb up. About halfway up, I lose my footing and almost crash to the ground. I press my face against the vines running up the terrace as I try to compose myself again.

Finally, I reach the roof, walk over, and peer through the windows, trying to determine which room is Tatum's. I find a bedroom and look around, examining it. It seems like it could be hers when I spot the Coffee Station apron in a laundry pile in the corner of the room.

Now the hope is that the window is unlocked. It is. Thank God. I slide the window open quickly and jump into the room, listening intently for the front door to open. Hopefully, they're having a backseat quickie and I have time.

I'm thinking too hard, I think to myself. I go to the laundry pile, lift some of the clothes, slide my knife and gloves underneath, and throw myself back out the window. I exit so hard I lose my footing again, only this time I'm unable to catch my balance. I roll down the roof and crash twenty feet down to the ground.

I cough as I try to bring the air back into my lungs. Breathing is difficult now, but only for a moment until the shock of the impact wears off.

"Cross that off the bucket list," I say. "Christ almighty."

I sneak around to the front of the house and see that Tatum's door is open. I panic. I have nowhere to run where she won't see me. I look around for an escape plan and think I'm caught when she suddenly slams the door closed again. I can see her looking in Cooper's direction and they're leaning in for a kiss. I lurk across the yard where Cooper can see me and stand and wait for a moment.

I make eye contact with him. His eyes widen as he sees me, though he can't fully see me. My silhouette is lit only by the porch light on the front of the house. I see him jump back and point at me. Now I have to run. I have to make a break for it. I dash out of sight and hide in trees dividing the property lines between houses.

I'm extra still, trying not to make a sound or move a branch on the trees; my body tangled in the branches like a fly caught in a spider web. I observe as Tatum gets out of the vehicle, walks up the sidewalk into her house, and closes the door. Cooper waits for her to make it to safety, gets out of the Volkswagen, looks around for a moment, then returns and drives off in the opposite direction of my home.

I walk back into my house and breathe a sigh of relief, then immediately head into the garage and fire up the bench grinder again. I open a drawer, pull out another Buck 119 Special, and begin sharpening it.

"This isn't over," I say aloud as though I'm talking to him, "it's only just begun.

CHAPTER 33
TOM LANGFORD

I finish sharpening the blade and this time it's got even more of an edge than the last one, the one I planted in Tatum's bedroom. I admire my work for a moment. This is the night. The night that the Knock Knock Killer makes a return. I'd planned for this, and I'd yearned for this. I want this. The fame of being a serial killer is unmatched; unfortunately, you're not really famous. Tons of people know of you, but they don't know you.

Staying in the shadows was always my goal growing up, and as I entered adult life, remaining in the shadows became even more critical. This is the life I chose, and I understand that. I'd rather be a ghost than be in the spotlight like Cooper. He likes the spotlight, though. He wants to be famous. He wants to be the guy that takes me down, and I won't let that happen.

I grab a fresh pair of black jersey gloves and slip them over my hands. Oops, I think. I wipe off the knife, realizing I had sharpened it without gloves. I think back to the knife I placed in Tatum's room, my stomach jumping up into my throat until I realized I was wearing gloves when I sharpened that one. I let out a deep breath.

I'd scoured the internet and various social media sites vigorously to find suitable targets for my next act of violence. I'd planned and planned, and that plan is in motion.

I chose the Roberts family. I needed a family with only three. There's the dad, John, the mom, Jane, and the son, Tyler. Kids were always the difficult ones, but once the parents were gone, I couldn't let them go into the system, which always fueled my zeal for blood.

I picked up my phone and sifted through the contacts until I found who I was looking for. I hit the call button and waited while it rang. It felt like it took forever, then the automatic voicemail voice popped through my end. No answer. I dial again. I can't do this without my partner. I need help, then an answer.

"Tonight is the night. Are you ready?" I say.

My partner confirms.

"Meet me at my house, and we will go from there," I say, confirming the plan, "their house is only two blocks over."

Tonight is the night. The night Cooper gets his final warning. The night he truly learns who he is fucking with. The night before the grand finale.

"There will be blood," I say out loud as I laugh.

CHAPTER 34

TOM LANGFORD

As I finish preparing for an eventful night, the first one I've had in years, I hear a knock on my front door. I grab the duffle bag and head to the front door, looking through the peephole before opening it, just in case. These days, you never know who might appear at your door and for what reason. The thought makes me laugh.

I don't want to kill again. I don't. Hand to god. That's really why I stopped for the last three years. I was done. My anger was tamed, and I felt good about life. I was ready to move on to a new me. The case was closed, and I knew I was safe to enter back in with the rest of society, but anger. Anger is a hell of an emotion. It makes you act out of impulse, and it makes you a different person.

The fact that this man-child decided to start sniffing around pissed me off. It pissed me off like a motherfucker, and I decided he would pay. He will pay for disturbing my life of peace. He will pay for the life I built that he stole from me. How will he pay? Monetarily? No. I have everything I need. I'm set financially. He will pay with his life. I will watch as life leaves his eyes.

I open the door and find my partner in crime standing on my front porch. A wide smile appears on my face as I make eye contact. I'm happy to be together again. No one else on this planet makes me nearly as comfortable. She smiles back—a genuine smile.

"I'm happy to see you, Tom," she says, "are you ready?"

I nod, then drop the duffle bag and throw my arms around her neck as she wraps me in a warm embrace. It's been three years since we called it off. It's been three years since we've seen one another. Cutting ties ultimately was the smart move. There was less of a chance of getting caught, but that didn't stop either one of us from sending a text here and there or chatting on the phone. It wasn't much, but it was better than nothing. At least I'd still run into her at the coffee shop here and there and I could lay eyes on her. The unfortunate part of that is we always have to pretend we don't know one another.

I still love her. She's all I can think about. I smell her hair as we hug, and all the feelings come back. Her hair smells like the same lavender vanilla shampoo that I remember from all those years ago. We back off, and I grab her by the waist and stare into her eyes for a moment. I can see it in her gaze. She hasn't stopped loving me, either.

I clear my throat, "Are you ready?" I say, though I already know the answer, "Thanks for coming out of hiding to help me. I appreciate it."

"If he implicates you, he implicates me," she says, "let's scare the shit out of him."

We're both a little out of practice so she sorts through my bag and I sort through hers, ensuring we have everything we need.

"Hey, I don't see your knife," I say, "do you need one?"

"Nope," she says as she pulls it out of her waistband and holds it up to show me.

"Hot."

She giggles that little schoolgirl laugh that I remember. Her face turns a bright pink with embarrassment, and she puts the knife away and hands me my duffle bag.

"I think you're all set," she says.

"You too," I hand her bag back to her.

I walk around the house, ensuring all lights are off, which seems silly, but at the moment, it's all I can do. There is always a moment before the kill that feels off when I almost consider staying home, but the adrenaline takes over, and I know that's only the start of a great night.

Tonight marks the beginning of the rest of my life.

CHAPTER 35
TOM LANGFORD

We pull up to the Roberts house. All seems quiet. It's always best to hit when they least expect it, though I don't think anyone ever expects this, especially after I've been on a hiatus for so long. The people of this town have their guards down, and that's a good thing. I always want to hit when they don't have a chance to attempt defensive measures.

We observe the home for a bit, taking it all in. I can see John clearing the table from what seems to be a relatively uneventful family dinner, and straight through to the kitchen where Jane is standing washing the dishes. As I look around, I can see a light flick on upstairs. That must be Tyler's room. I don't have a house layout, so it will be a guess and test hit, but once the parents are down, kids generally don't have a chance.

My stomach turns with nausea. The thought of killing a child always gets me, but this is how it must be. I extend my arm toward the glove box and reach inside, grabbing a bottle of Tums to quell the nauseous feeling. The nerves always get me right before a hit. That's why I keep them there, but that end result feeling. Oh, how I long for when my nausea finally subsides and the sense of a well-done job hits.

We circle the block so we can park one street over and walk through the neighbor's yards; we can't risk my car being seen. We park at the end of a cul-de-sac where the shining of the street lights don't touch, and we begin getting dressed. We put on our all-black garb, including our gloves and ski masks. The last thing we do is pull our hoods up over our heads.

We look at each other and smile. Though it's barely noticeable under the masks, I can see the wrinkles under her eyes as they light up, and she shoots me the smile I've longed to see. We stare at one another for a moment as we look deep into each other's souls, and as if we share a brain, we both lean in and kiss. A long, romantic, passionate kiss. Any of these hits could be our last, so we always shared a kiss beforehand and made love after. It's just our ritual, and I am glad she remembered.

"Let's do this," she says confidently, though I can hear her voice shaking.

I nod as I grab my knife and open my door. I close the door quietly. There is a house about fifteen to twenty yards away, and we can't risk them hearing. Any disturbance could alert any of the people in these houses, which would quickly become a bigger mess than it needs to be.

We run through the yards as fast as we can, yet as quietly as we can. Five houses down and two up. We hop the chain link fence into someone's backyard, and I immediately feel a squish under my foot. Ugh, dog shit. I continue to run until something stops me. I can hear a chain clanging, and I stop so abruptly that she almost slams into my back.

"What are you doing?" She asks me.

"Shh," I say with my finger up to my mouth.

I listen again, and suddenly I hear a growl, and in the dim light from the moon, I see a figure moving in the darkness. A german shepherd making its way toward us, the growling getting more and more intense as it begins to show us its teeth. We start to back away slowly, but the dog moves slightly faster than us to close the gap. I look back over my shoulder. We are only about twenty feet away from the fence at the back side of the yard. We can make it.

"On the count of three, run as fast as you can," I say.

We continue to back away slowly, also trying to close the gap between us and the fence.

Once we take off, the dog will run at us as fast as possible.

"One," I say, still moving backward, keeping my eyes locked on the dog.

"Two," She assumes the position to take off.

"Three," I yell, grabbing her and pushing her like it would give her some leverage to take off faster. As she runs, I keep my eyes locked on the dog, now snarling, showing more teeth, and almost foaming at the mouth.

The dog lunges forward at me and, at the same time, I unsheath my Buck 119, swinging it through the air and slamming the blade through the dog's side. With a yelp and a whimper, the dog falls to the ground panting heavily. No energy left in its muscular, gigantic body to attack.

"Down," I say with an arrogant look, "good boy."

I hop over the fence and run after her. She looks back to see me gaining ground on her and slows to a crawl. I also slow down, wiping the dog's blood off the knife. She notices and says, "Ah fuck, really? The dog?"

I nod. "Sorry," I say.

We slow-walk the rest of the way to the Roberts' house and come in through their backyard, which is not fenced in, which generally means they don't have a dog. Thank God. We get to the back corner of the house and press our backs to the siding, shimmying down the length of the home until we get to the front. We take one last look at one another, then round the corner.

I knock twice on the front door, my signature move, and after about fifteen seconds, no one comes to the door. The lights inside are on, but it's quiet. Almost too quiet. We look at one another, and we know what we have to do. We've come too far at this point to simply walk away. I try the door. Locked. I think for a moment, then back up a little bit, turn to the side, and slam my shoulder into the door. I hear a muffled scream inside the house as the door cracks slightly.

I examine it, which I should have done first, and luckily there is no deadbolt. Just one single lock to get past. It should break through the frame if I can hit it hard enough. Both of us back up a little this time, and at that exact moment, we slam our shoulders into the door, and it crashes open. Shards of wood go flying when the lock bolt breaks through like shrapnel on the battlefield.

I hear a scream again, louder this time, and a dish crashes to the ground and breaks into a thousand little pieces as Jane is stunned by the two people who just crashed through her front door. However, John is nowhere to be found, and I assume the worst; he's gone to get a gun. Jane is whimpering and cowering in the corner of the kitchen, frozen with fear.

We don't say a word as the two of us make our way toward her with knives out. The quaint tiny middle-class home is now a scene of terror as two masked intruders make their way toward the woman, ready to attack. Suddenly, a gunshot. A bullet whizzes past my head and hits a vase to the left of me. I look to my right and find John standing with an M&P Shield drawn and pointed directly at us.

"Don't move," he threatens, "don't move a fucking muscle."

I laugh audibly, and we turn our attention away from Jane and now to him. The man clearly is not a good shot, and he doesn't stand a chance with the two of us coming at him. However, we brought knives to a gunfight, and the irony isn't lost on me.

As we move in on him, he backs up, shakily holding the gun and pointing it at us. He doesn't do well under high-stress situations, and that's a good thing for us.

BANG!

Another shot goes off, narrowly missing me again. It's become clear that he's identified me as the more robust target. I can tell by the look in his eye and the muscles in his arms that he's about to squeeze the trigger again. I quickly drop to the ground and—

BANG!

Another shot. I don't know how many rounds he has in the gun, but he's used three. I'm on the ground still, and my partner distracts him. As he focuses on her. I crawl over to him, take my knife and slit right behind his heel, right at his Achilles tendon, and he drops like a sack of potatoes.

"Fuck," he cries out in agony as the ground becomes blood-soaked.

I grab the gun from him and stuff it in my waistband. No way I'm leaving it behind. I stand back up, and he looks at me, eyes wide, and begins begging for his life.

"No, please," he says, "I'll do anything," pleading with me, trying to negotiate a deal.

"Do you want money? I can give you money," he shouts.

I bend down to his level and look him dead in the eyes, "It's not about money," I say, "It's about sending a message."

I take the knife, hold it to his throat, and drag the blade across the length of it from left to right. He begins coughing and gagging as the blood pools up in his esophagus. It doesn't take long for his eyes to roll back into his head.

"Dad, what's going on down here?" A small voice says as Tyler descends down the stairs. He looks at me, down at the ground where his father is taking his last breath, then back at me with fear. I run up the stairs after him as he attempts to escape. I grab him by the ankles and drag him down the stairs into the kitchen, where Jane is still trembling in the corner of the room.

I grab him and throw him on the ground next to his mom. She grabs and holds onto him for dear life, fearing the worst. I bend down to their level and stare into their eyes. This fear is what I've longed for. The begging, the screaming, the crying. It gives me power. It gives me life.

"What do you want?" Jane asks through her tears.

I laugh sinisterly, then say, "What did I just tell your husband? I'm sending a message."

"To who?" She cries.

"Everyone," I say as I stab her in the neck repeatedly.

My partner handles Tyler next to me while I ensure Jane's life is fleeting. The two of us stand up, blood dripping down our sweaters. We smile at one another.

"Time to stage the bodies," I say to her.

"Already on it."

We line the bodies up in the foyer quickly. We can hear sirens in the distance. Whether they're coming for us is unclear, but one thing is sure: we don't want to be here much longer to find out. From left to right, we line them up, John, Tyler, and Jane, and quickly remove their clothing and carve words into their abdomens.

When the job is done, we take a moment to admire our work, but the sirens are getting louder and closer; it's time to take off. Someone saw us. Someone called the cops. It's time to go. We left them for the cops to find, though no trace of us ever being here will ever be found. This time, we left a note, a love letter, a little tip for the cops; we carved it right into our victims' bodies:

Cooper And Delilah

CHAPTER 36
TOM LANGFORD

The news spreads quickly, and headlines swiftly read:

Family of Three Dead, Is the Knock Knock Killer Back?

"All signs point to 'yes,'" I say, pointing and winking at the television with a glass of whiskey in my hand at one in the afternoon. I watch the news with pure joy, listening to the speculation and theories on what may have happened the night before. I laugh as though I was watching reruns of some early 2000s sitcom.

The news has changed a lot since I did this before. They don't hold back anymore, and they show everything from photos of the house to pictures of the bodies. But because of how we left them, certain portions were blurred and sometimes a police officer would step in front of the camera so the media couldn't get a good image.

Watching the footage, I don't tear my eyes away from the television for even a second; they finally announced it. Our message was scrolling across the bottom of the screen:

`Three Dead in Milan, Source Says Words Carved Into Bodies-Unconfirmed.`

They really don't hold back any of the details. I listen closely as the in-studio anchor makes an announcement, "Cooper Cobb and Delilah Carney, the pair that runs the popular 'Knock Knock Podcast,' allegedly could be to blame for the carnage that took place here last night," she said.

I spit out my drink. This is better than anything I could have hoped for. Cooper and Delilah are being blamed for my crime. How exciting. I let out a thunderous cackle as I imagine those two poor assholes being hauled away to jail. Would they be arrested and charged with murder? God, I hope so.

"Well, that's one way to get rid of them," I say as I take a sip of whiskey and kick my feet up on the foot rest on my recliner.

CHAPTER 37

TOM LANGFORD

My plan is coming together nicely. With Cooper and Delilah in jail, no one can stop me now. I make preparations for the next phase. This will go along without a hitch with them out of the picture. I won't have my partner next time, so I must plan accordingly. I have to plan for anything and everything. I must ensure that every second of the next hit is planned and perfectly thought out.

I sharpen three knives in the garage on the bench grinder this time. I have to make sure I have backups. With another person there to distract the targets, this will be easier. I could lose a knife. I could get taken down. I never know what I'm walking into, but especially this time. This time will be different.

I sip on my whiskey again, still enjoying the moment I saw the news covering their arrest. I watched as the two were walked out of their home in handcuffs and thrown into the back of a cop car. I watch as tears drip from Cooper's eyes and sadness pops through his usually cocky visage as they get hauled away to jail.

"The plan is coming together," I say as I sharpen yet another knife, "no one can stop me now."

I feel like Thanos when he finally gets his hands on all of the infinity stones. I smile. The power, the excitement, the adrenaline coursing through my veins.

"Time for a little reunion," I say.

CHAPTER 38

TOM LANGFORD

My jaw drops to the floor as I watch Cooper and Delilah's release coverage. The news says that they were only brought in for questioning and not officially charged or even accused of murdering the Roberts family. The plan did not come together as I imagined it would. To be fair, I never imagined them even being arrested, so now the police at least have someone they can watch. They can wait for another murder to happen, and the two of them will go back to jail, and, I promise, more blood will be shed.

According to the news, the police have no leads whatsoever, so whatever information Cooper has on me, he's withholding it from them. Why? Does he think he's going to take me down himself? The thought of him coming after me all by himself makes me laugh. The real kicker is he doesn't even know who I am. In due time, he will know me. He will see me. He will fear me.

I'm logged in to the live stream; Cooper and Delilah are about to start their weekly live show like they do every Friday, and I am more excited about this episode than I ever have been. I want to hear how he feared for his life when locked up, however brief that may have been. I want to listen to him say he's giving up. Giving up would be in his best interest.

I listen to the live show and it's the same old shit. Cooper sounds confident as ever, Delilah is her usual, slightly ditzy, slightly bothered-sounding self. He doesn't even mention their short stint in jail, probably trying to save face for his fans; he'd probably lose some if they knew he was arrested, though there's nothing permanent on his record. They move on to taking calls much quicker today than they have in the past — strange.

The standard calls come through; people professing their love for them and, for the show, a friendly little acknowledgement of support. Then another caller makes me stop what I'm doing and pay full attention to the show. He calls in, then after a moment, he sounds different. It sounds like they disguised his voice.

As he begins speaking, my heart sinks. He's telling them he was in front of the Roberts home the night before and watched us bust down the door. He's identified us, but only slightly. He's a great observer. He identified our genders without even seeing our faces.

Smart guy, too smart.

My grip on the whiskey glass tightens so much that the glass shatters under the force. Shards of glass land in my lap, and whiskey is everywhere. I get a rag and a broom to clean up the mess as I continue to listen. Cooper quickly ends the show and cuts the feed.

"Game on," I say.

CHAPTER 39
TOM LANGFORD

This weekend has been a whirlwind, and it's only Saturday. I'm watching the news again this morning and, if I'm being honest, that's one of the few things I do anymore. Even though I've been at peace for four years, not having to look over my shoulder, I still don't venture out into public often. Thank God for Instacart and Doordash or I'd have gone hungry a long time ago.

So to pass the time, I drink and watch the news; that's about it. Usually it's the same boring stuff we see all the time, like a shooting in Toledo or a hit-and-run in Cleveland. Lately, it's been much more exciting, but that's what happens when I get involved. Tatum, Cooper's newest crush is being escorted from her home in connection with the Roberts family murders. Police say they had a slew of evidence handed over, including what could potentially be the murder weapon, though they aren't saying where they got the knife from.

Cooper. I know the answer immediately, but it's not like I can call her and tell her who threw her under the bus. Maybe she already knows and maybe she is already planning his demise. I might not have to lift a finger, I think. I take a sip of whiskey. My only goal is to kill Cooper Cobb, but I'm hoping she does it for me now.

Today, I'm relaxing and chilling out; there is no reason for me to leave the house today. I heard that Cooper and Delilah are heading out of state to Michigan for some sort of stupid fucking show in front of a live audience. I think about it for a minute; I haven't been to Michigan in a hot minute. Maybe I should pay my friends a little visit out of state. Maybe I should ensure he knows that he isn't safe, not even when he leaves Ohio.

CHAPTER 40

TOM LANGFORD

I scour Facebook and Instagram to make sure I know exactly where they are going to be. The show is taking place at the Fox Theatre in Detroit. Ugh, Detroit, I think, but I'm making the trek anyway. It's not too far from us; only two hours, so the drive isn't bad, though I wasn't sure my car would make it there and back. I tried anyway and it did make it, surprisingly.

I stop at some random public parking lot just barely inside the downtown limits of Detroit and I get charged twenty bucks to park there. When the lot attendant approaches my vehicle and tells me that, I just about grab my gun and shoot him. Would that be too out of the norm for Detroit? I know the city has done a lot to clean up the streets so I choose to hand him the twenty and call it a day, but now I'm not leaving the parking lot so I'll have to walk.

I look at the Knock Knock Podcast Instagram and it looks like they've checked in at Greektown Casino for dinner; some restaurant called Pegasus Taverna. I have to look it up on Google Maps to find it. Luckily I'm only a five minute walk from there, and it's close to Halloween so I don't have to worry about my costume that conceals my identity. There's bound to be some Halloween night club party around here somewhere, I shouldn't be too out of place.

I get out of the car and take a look around. I don't see many people around me with the exception of the cars blasting down I-75 well over the posted seventy mile per hour speed limit. We don't dare do that in Ohio; the cops there aren't nearly as forgiving, but there are seemingly no laws on the road here. I walk around to the trunk of my car and open it. I don't have much gear with me; just a simple disguise. I don't plan on taking them down here.

I start walking down the street with everything on except my ski mask. People are friendly here, much friendlier than the news portrays them. Maybe I was wrong about this city. I can easily discern the out-of-towners, though, wearing their Detroit Lions and Tigers gear, stumbling over themselves piss drunk.

I find Greektown much easier than I anticipated and there is a sign outside showing that the Pegasus restaurant is just inside the doors. As I walk by, I do my best to blend in to the crowd and, as if some higher power is smiling down on me, I look over and see Cooper and Delilah sitting at a booth right in front of a window. I can't believe my eyes. They are right there. I escape down an alley quickly to put on my mask. I can't risk them seeing me; not yet, not here.

The mask is on and I'm ready to go. I peek around the corner and look inside the restaurant again. I see their waitress return with a couple of shots and they raise them and I can see Delilah talking as though she is making a toast. They take the shots and this is my moment. I pop out of the alleyway and stand on the sidewalk staring at them. The thought is to unnerve them, to make them nervous. Cooper looks over and spots me. I stand for a moment and when he turns away, blinking his eyes rapidly to make sure he's seeing me, I sneak away back into the alley and watch them again.

I can see Cooper panicking as he scans the street looking for me again, but I am nowhere to be found, at least to him.

"Perfect," I say out loud.

CHAPTER 41
TOM LANGFORD

I get to the will call box at Fox Theatre and I'm lucky enough to find that they have a handful of tickets left for the live show. I immediately buy one and they quickly sell out right after me. Good for them, I think, then I beat myself up inside my own head for being even that supportive of them and their stupid show.

When I enter the auditorium, even though there are plenty of seats left, I decide to stand against the wall in the back; less of a chance I'm spotted. They don't know what I look like and I intend on keeping that a secret for now. The program shows that they'll be doing their normal bullshit where they talk to one another and generally waste people's time, at least in my mind, but people are willing to listen.

The show starts and they drone on and on and it feels like it will never end. I'm waiting for the Q&A session at the very end. That's where I will strike fear in their hearts, that's where I will make them panic. He already knows, or at least he thinks he knows he isn't safe, even here, but I want to put him into a complete meltdown.

***

The intermission is almost over and they will be taking the stage again to start the Q&A session and my nerves are starting to get the best of me. The venue is packed with over five thousand people and it will only take one to chase me down, tackle me and it's over; my life, the plan, everything will be shot to hell. I have to be ready for anything.

They take the stage and the crowd is losing their minds raising their hands wanting to ask them questions. The first person they call on, a guy toward the front, asks them what they're going to do if the killer, i.e. me, comes after them. I snicker to myself, but I'm also wondering if Cooper will answer honestly. To my surprise he does. He tells the whole crowd about the threats I've been sending him and the warnings he's received. Hearing him say it makes me laugh a little harder, because even though he's trying to sound brave, I can hear the fear in his voice.

The next person they call on, someone toward the back of the crowd asks them what their plan is since they don't know who I am. I feel a sense of pride when he asks this question, because even though I've been messing with them, they still have no clue who I am. Cooper responds in that arrogant tone that he uses on the podcast. That fucking annoying, cocky edge to his voice pisses me off. He tells the man they will find me and they will kill me. The answer makes me laugh even harder, but I also see this as my chance so I need to find my composure and make sure they look at me. I'm going to say something.

When they call on someone else, my hand shoots up in the air faster than I intended for it to and my mask isn't even on fully, but just as I planned, they call on me. The guy standing in the aisle next to me hands me a microphone and now that I'm standing here with it in my hand, I partially freeze up for a minute. I didn't plan this far ahead. What am I going to say? I need to buy some time. As soon as I speak, I need to get the hell out of here.

"What's your question, sir?" says Delilah, her sweet voice breaking the silence among the crowd.

"Hello, Cooper and Delilah," I say, filling my words with the most terrifying tone I can, I drop my voice in pitch and make it sound like I swallowed a ton of glass and I say the first thing that comes to mind.

"Knock, Knock."

As soon as the words leave my mouth, I throw the microphone to the ground and take off to my right. I noticed an emergency exit sign earlier and had already decided that was my escape route. As I take off running, I can hear the feedback from my microphone hitting the floor coming through the speakers. Then I hear it again and I look behind me and I see Cooper jumping off the stage and running down the aisle after me. He knows it's actually me now and I should have planned for this better, but I didn't and now I have to think on my feet.

I crash through the emergency exit door and look left, then right, then left again. I have maybe five seconds to hide or he will find me, tackle me to the ground and probably beat the ever-loving shit out of me and I am without a weapon. I look to the right again and notice people walking past the theater. I charge for the street and run out to blend in with the crowd, taking off my mask in the process. As soon as I hit the sidewalk and turn, out of sight, I can hear Cooper yelling, "Come and get me you pansy ass mother fucker."

I blend in well with the crowd and I walk away, smiling.

PART 3

CHAPTER 42
COOPER COBB

The chaos from the weekend is over, and now we have time to reflect on everything that's happened. With our evidence turned over to the police, we both feel a little beaten down. They have the photos that I dissected. They know about the size thirteen boot print, and the caller on the podcast that told us there are two people involved. They know about the knife, and, worst of all, they know about Tatum. They brought her in for questioning yesterday but, since we were out of town, we didn't hear too much about it. If she did play a part in all of this, she might be long gone by now.

Delilah has herself holed up in her room. She doesn't want to talk; I've never seen her this upset. Yesterday, she was fine, but I think that was just a facade. Usually, she leans on me as her rock. Today, I'm the enemy. Today, I'm the one that gave in. I think she feels like I gave up when I handed it all over to the detectives. I haven't, though. Now that they have some information, it's a race against the clock, it's a race against the killer before he strikes again, and it's a race against the police department.

I walk up to Delilah's bedroom door and tap on it twice.

"Go away," she says, "I don't want to talk to you."

"I'm just letting you know that I'm going to see my parents today. Do you want or need anything before I get back home?"

"No," she says, followed by silence behind the door.

"Thank you," I say, "for Friday night. It was nice and with all the craziness I didn't get to tell you."

CHAPTER 43
COOPER COBB

The drive over to my parents is tranquil. It's a relaxing, though not particularly long, drive; it's nice to have some time inside my own head. To some, it may be a curse, but I find it to be a blessing. To get to their house, it's just a quick drive out of town down Route 113 into Berlinville. The portions of the road offering the most peace are the cornfields. As I drive, I observe some deer running and jumping through the field, once full of life, now a barren wasteland of broken corn stalks after the farmers have already taken their combines to it.

The peace is a welcome visitor after the months of hell I'd put myself in. I did this to myself, and I can acknowledge it, but the mystery must be solved, and the Knock Knock Killer must be stopped for good. I can't—no, I won't let him murder anyone else, even if it's the last thing I do.

Here I go again, thinking of the man that's taken so much from me. My everyday life is gone, though maybe there's no one I can blame but myself. I did this, not him. He may have murdered all those people, but I'm the one who chose to obsess over it. I'm the one who decided I could be the savior. I'm the one who put off relationships and friendships and ended my relatively dull life in exchange for the life of an amateur detective, one that is ineffective at their job.

Maybe I'm no better than the police. Perhaps I just don't understand what exactly goes into that job. I mean, I've had many sleepless nights poring over documents and evidence to find what? A boot print? The knife was a coincidence; I know that. It was the right place, right time sort of thing, but that's precisely what makes me believe in fate. If I hadn't been in the coffee shop that day or hadn't struck up a conversation with Tatum or chosen to ask her out, I'd have never found it. Maybe that's what it will take to bring the killer to justice, being in the right place at the right time.

I need to be everywhere and nowhere all at once. I need to maneuver, I need to slink, I need to be a ghost. I need to become him. I need to get into his mindset to figure this out. He could be anywhere. He could be watching me right now. I glance around and in my rearview mirror as I drive. There is a car behind me, about a quarter mile down the road. Could it be him?

I shake the feeling off. Now I'm being paranoid. He doesn't leave town. He strikes when you least expect it, and only in Milan. He's never deviated from that formula. Maybe that's the twist. Perhaps he will strike elsewhere. Maybe he's figured out what I have and that he needs to change it up to keep things fresh, to keep us guessing.

I pull into the driveway as I arrive at my parent's house. They still live in my childhood home, and sometimes I come here to escape from reality. Just a short visit with them can make everything better, most times. If I know my mom as well as I think I do, she's already firing up the coffee pot after seeing me pull in, and she's frantically running around the house, wondering if it's clean enough at the same time. My dad will be sitting in the recliner with a beer in his hand, yelling at her, "Janice, it's your son, not a dinner party. Relax," which makes her clean even more feverishly with the frustration of being told to relax.

I get out of the car and take a deep breath. The fresh air that comes with being in the country brings me back to my childhood and relaxes me. I look out across the road into the field. I can see more deer frolicking near the tree line without a care in the world. They don't know it, but hunting season will be starting soon. Their life of carelessness turns into a horror movie itself. As I turn to go inside, the vehicle behind me slows to a crawl, and I make eye contact with the driver as he passes. He steps on the gas as he realizes I notice him.

CHAPTER 44

DELILAH CARNEY

```
Make him stop, or else…
```

It's a warning that sends chills up my spine, especially when it comes from a number I don't recognize, even though I know who it is. I stare at my phone as I lie in bed with the cursor blinking, waiting for a reply; then, another message pops through:

```
…I'll kill you.
```

I want to text Cooper, but I know he's upset with me. He's upset because I'm upset, and it's understandable. I should be more understanding. I should have known it would come to this at some point. If I had come to terms with it much sooner, it would have been easier to process.

I just didn't want him to hand over everything to the police. While I know he has copies of everything, this feels like a setback. I lie in my bed and cry. I cry for him. I cry because I feel like we're starting over. I cry because, no matter how platonically I try to live with him, the longer we are together, I fall harder and harder, making all of this much more difficult.

I want to hold him, comfort him, and tell him everything will be okay, but, to sound convincing when you tell someone that, you have to believe it yourself. I don't believe it. I don't believe one fucking syllable of that because deep down, I know that nothing will ever be okay again.

CHAPTER 45
TOM LANGFORD

"Fuck you, Cooper Cobb," I yell as I speed down the road, pushing the upper limits of what my car can handle.

The tracker notified me that Cooper was on the move and I need to know where he is. I need to know his movements and whereabouts at all times. We are too close for this to get messed up now. I speed around a curve and land myself on Route 113, pushing the gas with such ferocity the vehicle shudders as I move it past its limits.

Speeding down the highway, I see no sign of him, just empty farm field upon farm field, houses scattered here and there. I look at my phone to confirm he's still on Route 113. Yes. He is. I can see my indicator flashing on the screen, then scroll up, keeping an eye on him, all the while trying to keep my vehicle in its lane as it fights me on the speed and stress I'm putting it under.

I'm catching up now and just barely, about a quarter of a mile up the road. I see him. That stupid pink Volkswagen; god, do I hate that car. Of course, it's my fault he's driving it. I laugh, remembering the massive hole I put in his tire. Just barely trailing now, my car is shaking like a leaf and it feels like it will fly right off the frame if I hit the brakes too hard. I start to tap on them. I can't make it look like I'm following right behind. I distance myself from him again.

I watch as he makes a sharp left turn into a driveway, and he stops. I slow the car down to just barely a crawl. I'm watching intently as I pull up to the house. He opens his door, gets out, and looks right at me as I pass the house. We make eye contact, and I forget why I'm there for a moment. When panic sets in, I step on it and floor it out of there, but not before I notice the name on the mailbox reads: "Cobb."

He's seen me.

He knows my face now.

He knows who he is messing with.

Does he really know who I am?

I drive about another mile up the road, giving him time to go inside so I can sneak away. Unfortunately, I have to make a U-turn ahead and come back. It's the only way back into Milan. I make my U-turn and carefully drive back up to the house. No sign of him. I let out a huge breath. I must have been holding it and didn't realize it.

Just as I am passing the house, my car begins to chug. I hit the gas to get out of there, but it hesitates. It won't move. White smoke is pouring out of the engine compartment, and I slowly come to a stop.

Rolling.

Rolling.

Dead.

Right in front of what I'm now assuming to be his parent's home, the little bastard is inside.

CHAPTER 46

COOPER COBB

I walk into the house, and my mom immediately runs up and throws her arms around me in a warm maternal embrace. I throw my arms around her as well. My mom is one of the strongest, most amazing women I've ever met.

Immediately I can smell coffee and see my dad in the living room, sitting in his recliner, beer in hand. Called it, I think. Mom won't let go and it feels like she is squeezing the life out of my body. I know why, though. I get it. My name has been flying out of the mouths of those pesky news anchors a lot lately, and with my short stint in jail, I understand her protective side taking over.

She lets go of me finally, and I make my way into the kitchen, pouring myself a cup of coffee, allowing the aroma to fill my nostrils and wake me up. I take a sip and nearly burn the hell out of my tongue, but still, it tastes so good.

I walk into the living room next to my dad. He is watching the news, and I get sucked into the report. They're showing footage of a house I recognize, though I've only seen it in the dark.

```
Suspect Arrested in Connection With Knock
Knock Killer.
```

The banner reads along the bottom of the screen almost simultaneously as the footage rolls of police pulling Tatum out of her home in handcuffs. It hurts me in the deepest depths of my heart to know I did this to her, but if she is involved, I know it's a good thing. The news doesn't know about my involvement, thankfully. The detectives agreed to keep their source confidential, though I know that Tatum knows it was me.

I sit on the couch and continue to sip my coffee, and mom sits next to me with her own mug in hand. The three of us stay silent for a few minutes, continuing to watch the news coverage. It's surreal to think that maybe I caught the killer, or at least his accomplice. As I'm engrossed in the television, I hear an engine backfire outside that makes me jump out of my skin. My dad looks over and through the front window and chuckles to himself.

"Someone just broke down outside," he says.

I look over and see a car sitting on the side of the road outside, white smoke pouring out of the engine. I examine the vehicle for a moment. It looks like the same car that passed me as I was heading inside. I shake the thought off and don't think about it again.

"So," I say, trying to break the silence, "What's up?"

"We should be asking you the same thing," my dad says, pointing at the TV, "did you do this?"

My cheeks go red with a mix of embarrassment and shame. I don't want to be the one, but the fact is, I am. I did get her thrown into jail. Less than thirty-six hours ago, we were having some of the best sex of my life, and now? Off to jail she goes. It would be my luck that I fell for a serial killer.

"Yeah," I say, waiting for them to lecture me about being safe and not getting involved.

"Well," he says, "I'm proud of you." The vote of confidence shook me to my core. This wasn't to be expected at all.

I look over at my mom, who I can see physically shaking. I know why. She's worried about me. She worries more than dad does, for sure. She never wanted me to get involved. She found out about the podcast and lectured me for hours about it. Like a rebellious child, however, I did it anyway.

"Mom," I say, putting a hand on her shoulder, "I know you're worried. You don't need to worry anymore. It's over."

"I have a bad feeling," She says, "it's not over. Something tells me this isn't the person you're looking for." She points at the TV.

"Mom, she had the murder weapon in her room."

"What were you doing in her room?" She asks, accusatory.

Dad chimes in with, "that's my boy," as he takes a swig of his Bud Light, then laughs.

"Her and I dated briefly, but," I say, gesturing toward the TV, "clearly, that's over with."

Mom begins shaking even more. The thought had occurred to me that maybe Tatum wasn't the one I was after, that, perhaps somehow, sometime, the murder weapon was planted in her room to frame her. Perhaps this is precisely what the killer wants. Maybe he wants to take any attention off of him. Perhaps he's going to strike again.

The thought sends chills up my spine. Where will he strike? When will he strike? He's broken his pattern now. There's no telling what will happen next. It chills me to the bone, but I try not to focus on it. I want to focus on what's in front of me. Still, the thought is haunting me.

CHAPTER 47

DELILAH CARNEY

Depression has set in. I can feel it. I can feel it all around me. I still haven't pulled myself out of bed. I can't. I won't. I feel paralyzed. Fear, depression, and anxiety is hanging in the air around me. No matter how hard I try, I can't find the motivation to get up. The killer's words are hanging in the air around me. I'll kill him. Thinking about him dying makes my whole body tense up.

I know I've fallen for him. I shouldn't have, but I love him. How did I think men and women could live together platonically? I've known him forever. I know he's the one. I can't stop the thoughts. I want him. I need him. Physically and emotionally. I want to feel his body on mine. I want to hold him. Forever.

The killer sends another message.

I'll make you watch as his insides spill on the floor. Make. Him. STOP.

I can't. I won't. Keep going, Cooper. You can do this, I think to myself. Hunt him down, Cee. Kill this mother fucker.

CHAPTER 48

TOM LANGFORD

So here I sit on the side of the road, right in front of their house, "Fuck," I yell as I slam my hands on the steering wheel. The white smoke is still billowing out of the engine. Blown transmission. Damnit. Think, Tom, Think. They had to have seen it; someone would be coming outside any minute. Cooper is too good of a person to ignore someone in trouble. I hate him.

I pop the hood and get out of the car. It's the only thing I can do right now. I don't know anything about cars, but I know I can't drive it back home. I know I'm stranded here. I'm full of regret for once in my life. I shouldn't have followed him. I'm blankly staring at the engine, though the issue is further underneath where I can't see it.

I look toward the house. Nothing. No movement. Panic is blinding me. He doesn't know me from Adam, though. He doesn't know who I am. To him, I'll be a stranger. I haven't been this close to him. Then I hear the squealing of old hinges, and I look over. Through the smoke, I can see a figure standing in the doorway.

"Sir, do you need help?" I hear Cooper yell over to me. This is my chance. It's my chance to take him down once and for all. I'll kill the parents, too, if I need to.

CHAPTER 49
COOPER COBB

I zone out, staring out the window; the man on the side of the road is still sitting in his car as thick smoke continues to billow out of the engine. I should go see if he needs help. The news is still playing, but that's expected. Dad rarely watches anything else. I could ask if we could change it and watch a movie or something, but that would be a waste of breath. It's 24/7 news coverage in this house, especially since the changeover on the show. Sometimes I think he expects me to turn up dead.

A banner streams across the bottom of the screen again, but this time it reads something haunting, unexpected, and eerie:

`Milan Woman Released From Police Custody, No Charges at This Time.`

Did I wrongly accuse her? There must not be enough evidence to hold her. Either she's not guilty, or she's just that good. My hands begin to shake, the coffee sloshing in the cup. If she is involved, I just opened up a new can of worms for us. I jump up from the couch, and dad looks at me from his recliner, a slightly concerned look on his face, but not enough to put mom into a panic.

"Well, son," he says, "good luck with that."

He laughs it off, but this is no laughing matter. This is bad. This is dangerous. I need to get out of here. I need to go home. I need to protect Delilah. She might go after her. If she is who I think she is, she's dangerous. I jump up from the couch, leaving my coffee mug on the side table. This is bad. This is very, very bad, I think.

"I-I have to go."

I run to the front door without so much as a wave to my parents. As I look across the yard, I'm reminded of the man parked out front. He has his hood up, looking down into the engine. I can't just leave. If I drive by him without a single word then I look like an asshole.

"Sir, do you need help," I yell across the yard, though I hope he says no or that he has a tow truck on the way already.

"Oh, yeah, thanks," he says as I walk toward him, a dejected and embarrassed look on his face.

"Can you give me a ride to my house in Milan?" He says with an awkward smile.

"Sure, that's actually where I'm headed."

"Thanks," the man says, reaching out for a handshake, "I'm Tom. Tom Langford. A pleasure to meet you."

"Cooper, nice to meet you too," I say as I hold my hand out and shake his.

CHAPTER 50

DELILAH CARNEY

I found motivation. Not much, but I found it, and not in the way I expected. I'm still in bed but sitting up now. It's a step in the right direction, but it's not because I wanted to. It was reflexive. I received another text. This one is worse than the previous two. This time it's a photo. The cursor in the text message app is blinking rapidly at me, expecting a response, but I can't find the words to respond. I can't find them. I need to run, I need to get out of here, I need to—shit, Cooper has my car.

I'm staring at the message. I can only do so much. It's from the killer. It's from him, and it's a photo. I can see Cooper's parent's house in the background and my bright pink Volkswagen in the driveway. The picture is slightly slanted, as if it was taken with haste. The killer is with Cooper. The killer is right behind him, taking his photo. What's the story here, though? I press and hold the image, hoping it was taken as a live photo. It is, so it plays a quick video of the moments leading up to the photo being taken. Cooper says, "Go ahead, Tom, get in."

"Get in?" I yell. That's enough to make me jump out of bed, though I'm still not sure what I will do or how I will get there. I need to do something. I need to help. I need to make sure he's safe, but I'm stuck. I have to sit here in my own head with my own thoughts. I can't call him. I won't risk that. Should I call the Knock Knock Killer?

I need to hope.

I need to pray.

I need him to be okay.

CHAPTER 51
COOPER COBB

The trip from Berlinville to Milan, while a short trip, feels like the longest journey of my life. The atmosphere inside the car is tense. I glance from the corner of my eye a couple of times, and Tom's hands are balled up into fists, because of the issues with his car, I assume. We don't talk much, and all he says to me are directions to his home.

He lives about four blocks away from Delilah and me, yet I have never seen him. Milan is a tiny town with a population of only about 1,400 people. It's one of those places where it feels like you're constantly repeatedly running into the same people.

We pull up to his house, and he simply gets out of the car. As he goes to close the door, he leans back in, looks at me, and says, "Thanks, Cooper. I hope to see you soon." The smile on his face is weak, forced, and a little sinister. I try not to look for a deeper meaning within it.

"No problem," I say. I can feel a slight suspicion in my appearance, and I quickly try to get rid of it. He slams the door shut.

***

I head up the walkway leading to our front door. I regret having nothing in my hands for Delilah. I should have bought her a Monster Energy or something like that. I know she's still upset with me. She holds onto grudges tighter than anyone else I have ever met. I look back at her car, considering going back out and grabbing something for her. She did say not to get her anything, though.

I grab the door handle, and the door is pulled open faster than I can push it. Delilah jumps up, and I have to throw my arms out quickly to grab onto her to avoid her body crashing into the ground. It doesn't matter; as her body and mine make contact, she wraps her legs around my waist and arms around my neck to catch herself.

She takes me by surprise when she repeatedly begins kissing me on the stoop; my face is wet with what I assume to be tears streaming down her face. She leans back so I can look at her and her at me. I don't know what happened while I was gone for her to act like an overly excited golden retriever as soon as I returned, but I'm okay with it.

I love her. This much is clear now. Not only do I love her, but I'm also in love with her. I grab her face, stare into her eyes, and admire her. I run my fingers through her hair, then lean in and give her another quick kiss.

"I love you, Delilah," I say, which takes her by surprise, and the tears begin streaming down her face again. She grabs me and pulls me in, and holds me tight.

"I'm so sorry, Cooper," she whispers in my ear through stifled sobs.

"For what?"

She pulls away and stares at me, wiping the tears from her eyes.

"I-I can't," as she turns around and returns to her bedroom with a door slam.

CHAPTER 52
COOPER COBB

`Fuck you, Cooper. You're a piece of shit.`

Over and over again, the messages come through from Tatum. The same message is copied and pasted again and again and again. I am convinced that I've entirely screwed myself out of any intimate relationship with both of the women I've ever loved. It's been four days since Delilah talked to me, other than quick texts back and forth, but today is recording day, so she needs to speak with me for the show. Even if that's the case, I'll be happy for her to talk to me again.

I don't know if I did something wrong. I think I took her off guard a little bit by telling her I love her, but it's not like it was a first date. Maybe it was how quickly things progressed. We'd never honestly discussed if we fell for each other somewhere along the lines of us living together, and the only time we agreed to marry was if we hit forty years old and were still unmarried. Now, I'm not sure she will even be in my life. I wish I knew what she's doing in her room all day. Is she looking for a new place to live? Is she researching ways to kill me and hide my body?

I need some closure on the issue. What are we doing? She kissed me. She kissed me passionately.

I sit at the dining room table and stare into space, thinking about everything that's gone wrong over the last few days. I'd considered texting Tatum back, but she won't listen, I'm sure. Still, having no resolution, no closure on anything in life right now, is driving me to insanity. I need something.

I received another text this morning. Not from Tatum nor from Delilah. From the Knock Knock Killer. It's become a regular thing and doesn't send chills down my spine anymore. It just pisses me off; the constant threats are annoying now and just fuel the fight in my soul. I'm going to take him down. He's taken everything from me and doesn't even know it.

I hear a door open down the hall, and I think Delilah will finally make an appearance. She walks out to the kitchen and sits down across from me. She doesn't make eye contact with me, but I can practically hear her thinking.

"I'm sorry," she says after a minute, still looking down at the table, "I'm sorry."

She repeats it again and again, and I stare at her, not knowing what to say. I've thought a lot about our first encounter after this little hiatus, but I didn't prepare for her to apologize like she is. I reach across the table and grab her hand, rubbing it lightly with my thumb to show her everything is okay.

"No, I'm sorry," I say, "I shouldn't have come on so strong. I was caught up in the moment."

"That's the thing. I wanted to say it back. I couldn't."

"Why not?"

"I just. I do love you. I really do."

"Can you ever see us being…a thing?" I ask.

Her cheeks turn light pink as I ask, and I know exactly what her answer will be. She cracks a smile, then finally looks up at me. "Yes," she says, and at that moment, I know everything will be okay. I know we will get through this together.

"You know I have to try to make up with Tatum, right?" I say.

Her expression drops slightly, but she nods and says, "I know."

"If I can get her to agree, she might make a good guest interview on this Friday's live episode."

Delilah nods in agreement again. It's all about the numbers. If we can advertise it on the recorded episode on Friday morning, the live show may explode with listeners. It sounds like a terrible way to apologize, but it may allow her to find redemption and share her story. Of course, I would also have to explain to our listeners how I was wrong. I cringe at the thought. Suddenly, my phone begins vibrating on the table, and we both look at it. It's a text from Unknown.

`You fingered the wrong person, Cobb…`

Yeah, no shit. Then another text pops up.

`…but you're close. Soon.`

Delilah and I look at one another, then she says, "What does he mean by 'you're close'?"

I shake my head, "I don't know."

CHAPTER 53
COOPER COBB

"...If you're listening to this, come and get me; I'm ready for you," I say before signing off, "This has been the Knock Knock Podcast with Cooper Cobb,"

"And Delilah Carney."

I end the recording session. I'm done with the games, and I'm done with the **B.S.** If the Knock Knock Killer wants me, he will have to come for me. Not my family, not my friends. Let's see if he has the balls to come for me. I have enough rage inside me that I think I could take him down on pure adrenaline alone.

Earlier today, I got Tatum to calm down a bit before coming to record, and she agreed to meet me. Thankfully. Hopefully she and I can try to come to some understanding. I'll plead my case, try to get her to see things my way, and maybe, just maybe, she will understand. I imagine getting her to understand won't be easy, but I'll do my best. We need her on the show on Friday. We need her to share her side of the story, and we need her to be in the studio with us.

We filled our listeners in on all the different things that had happened over the last week and even told them we could have a surprise guest on the show and they needed to tune in. We can't let them down. We can't. We won't.

Delilah has agreed to come with me when I meet up with Tatum. She can act as a bodyguard for me. The thought is laughable, but I need the support. Maybe a female comrade is precisely what she needs there; someone who can see things from a woman's perspective but also, as my friend, and help her see things the way I see them. The way we see them. Delilah also agrees that we can't be too trusting of Tatum. We have to keep our guard up. Until we hear some sort of valid explanation as to why the knife was in her room, we can have no trust in her.

I look at my phone. 4:47 p.m. We are supposed to meet Tatum at 5:30 at the coffee shop. A public meeting would be ideal so that if she tries anything, there will be witnesses and potential backups to help us out. We have two days until showtime, so there is no time to waste. If we are going to draw the killer out of hiding, we need the one person who has been suspected of the crimes.

CHAPTER 54

COOPER COBB

We get to the Milan Coffee Station a little earlier than anticipated, which is fine because I want some time to get a coffee. Coffee is one of my few crutches, and it calms me down… somehow. Addiction is funny like that.

Delilah and I sit in a booth in the back of the restaurant and devise a game plan. We both realized we had never discussed how we would approach the situation and determined that the best course of action was for me to apologize first.

Deepening in our discussion, I feel a tap on my shoulder and turn around.

"Riley," I say, "hey dude, what are you doing here?"

"I saw Delilah's car outside and thought I would pop in for a second and say hi."

I can see on Riley's face that he's concerned about us, but he will never say it. He knows I will brush it off and tell him everything is fine and not to worry.

"I've seen the news," he says, "what's the story there?"

"A long one," I say, trying to keep him as uninvolved in our drama as possible. He's a good friend. I've known him for a long time. He doesn't deserve to get dragged into the mess we've created, and I don't intend on giving the Knock Knock Killer another target to go after. I know once he hears the Friday episode, it will be game over. Once he hears me baiting the killer, I know he will be on my ass.

"I don't want to get you involved," I reassure him, "It's not that I don't want to tell you."

"I understand."

The front door to the coffee shop opens, and I see Tatum walking in. Riley must have seen my eyes dart to the door because he turns around and looks. He turns back, looks at us, eyes wide, and says, "Whelp, I'm getting the eff out of here." He turns around and walks away, bumping into Tatum as he passes her.

"Watch it," she says.

"Hey, try not to kill my friends over there," he says.

I facepalm as he gives me a thumbs up, walking out the door.

"Hi," Tatum says to us.

"Hi," we say in unison, awkwardly.

"Do you want–" I say, gesturing at the counter, but she cuts me off mid-sentence.

"I'm fine."

She sits down next to me. I can see her eyes are filled with sadness. She regrets being with me that night. She regrets ever meeting me, and I can see that she is embarrassed doing this at her job. She tries to hide it, but I can feel the sorrow radiating off of her, and I feel bad because I know I caused it. We don't have time to waste, so I jump right into it.

"First, thank you for meeting us," I start. Tatum nods without saying a word. "Second, I'm sorry."

Her posture straightens as I say the words, showing me that's all she wanted to hear. The glassy look in her eyes begins to clear up a little bit, and she wipes one last tear from her face. Delilah reaches over and grabs her hand showing a vote of support, showing her that we are with her and that we believe her, even though I'm the one that put her in that mess in the first place.

"I was hoping," I start, but I catch Delilah shooting me a look, "we were hoping you might join us on the show Friday evening. You know, to tell your side of the story."

Suddenly, Tatum's eyes light up like a kid who just walked into one of those old-timey candy stores. The pure joy emanating from her is contagious and even makes us smile.

"That would be wonderful," she yells, catching herself and looking around to find other patrons staring at her.

"Oops," she says, "got a little too excited."

Delilah and I share in happiness with her. The conversation goes on for hours and hours, and before we know it, we are laughing and joking, and we all agree to put everything behind us that's happened over the last four days. To an outsider, you might think we are three friends that haven't seen one another in a long time, catching up on life and enjoying each other's company.

I lose track of time and finally look down at my phone. 9:08 p.m.

"Holy shit, we need to go. We have to do a little planning for Friday evening," I say.

As the three of us get up to leave, Delilah walking about five steps ahead of us, I stop and grab Tatum's hand. We stop, and Delilah walks out the front door, realizes we aren't behind her anymore, and looks back through the window. She throws her hands up in the air in a "what the hell" sort of motion, and I hold a finger up, telling her to give me a minute. I turn Tatum toward me to look her in the eyes, and she grabs my other hand.

"I want you to know I truly am sorry," I say, unintentionally giving her sad puppy dog eyes.

She blushes, then says, "I know you are; I can hear it in your voice."

"It's just," I start, "It was right there. In your room."

"I know, I get it, and I'm sorry for calling you a piece of shit," she says, "over and over and over again."

She doesn't know that I do feel like the biggest piece of shit in the world right now. I jumped to conclusions, and unfortunately, I was wrong. I don't think I'll ever be able to make it up to her, and I don't think there is a future for us, except maybe as friends, but that's it. If I got back with her, I can almost guarantee Delilah wouldn't forgive me. She would probably move out, never to be heard from again since I think, maybe, we are a thing now? I'm not sure. Something we need to talk about.

"So," she says, moving closer to me, wrapping her arms around me, "is there a chance we can start over?"

I audibly gulp as the question takes me off guard. I didn't imagine she would be the one asking me, and I need to devise an excuse as quickly as possible. I've fallen for Delilah, and she's my best friend. There isn't any tension between us like I can feel between Tatum and me.

"I don't know right now," I say, "I need to do some introspection before I jump back into a relationship, I think."

She looks disappointed but nods in agreement. I know she understands. I know that she knows I feel terrible for what I put her through.

"I get it," she says, "well, when you're ready." She smiles at me. I know everything is going to be okay.

CHAPTER 55

COOPER COBB

"We need to do something big, something dramatic… something to pull him out of hiding," I say as Delilah and I make plans for Friday's big live event. In less than 48 hours, we would be doing everything in our power to ensure the Knock Knock Killer is no more, even if it means we have to kill him with our bare hands. We need a foolproof plan for this to work. We must be sure that we anger him enough to make him come after us.

I intend on this being the end of him. The end of his rage and the end of his massacres. I glance at the clock as we obsessively sort through all the evidence we have on him. 3:08 a.m. We should be in bed, sleeping, but the adrenaline coursing through our veins is too much. Even if we did lie down, we would stare at the ceiling all night, wasting time. We need to do this, and it needs to be perfect.

While I scour every file we have, clicking "print" on every crime scene photo, Delilah sits on the floor, sorting, compiling, and making a timeline of events. We still don't know who he is, and I intend to find out before the show. I plan on calling him out by his real name and not the words that strike fear into the hearts of this community.

Less than 48 hours, I think, but how do you name a ghost? How do you identify someone who can't be identified? You hunt them down.

Suddenly, the sound of glass shattering makes the two of us jump. A photo that Delilah is holding goes flying across the room and sticks to the wall. We look at one another, then look at the picture. We can see something shiny sticking out of the wall. We walk closer to it and investigate. A Buck 119 Special is sticking out of the wall and right through the head of the victim in the photo. I grab it and pull it out of the wall. It flew through the window and almost hit Delilah right in the head.

I inspect the knife, immediately knowing this is a warning from him. Nothing is too unordinary about this knife except for one thing. This one is just slightly different from the one you would order online. This one is customized. At the bottom of the blade, just above the handle, there are initials laser etched into the knife. He made a mistake. A detrimental mistake to himself. He just told us everything we needed to know.

"Look," I say to Delilah as I point to the bottom of the metal.

"Holy shit," she says.

The initials read "T.L." Delilah looks at me, horrified. We have initials now. This is the closest we have ever been to finding the truth.

"What does T.L. stand for?" Delilah asks.

I think about it for a few moments, rubbing my finger over the engraving. I almost zone into my thoughts and let the world disappear. I know the answer, though I don't want to say it. I was close. I was so close, and I didn't realize it. I snap out of my stupor and look at Delilah with fear, realizing my life could have ended, and I had no clue. I stare her in the eyes for a moment, and she can see that somehow, someway, I know the answer.

"Tom Langford," I say.

PART 4

CHAPTER 56

TOM LANGFORD

Friday night. 9 P.M. It's on.

The text flashes on my iPhone. It's game time. Cooper is going live tomorrow evening at nine, and it's finally time to take him down once and for all. His game is over. I'm done with him. I'm over the bullshit. I check and recheck my duffle bag to ensure everything is in order. I can't miss a step, and I can't miss a single minute.

Gloves. Check.

Mask. Check.

Knives. Check.

I go over the list again and again. It's time to put this boy in his place. It's time to truly show him who he is messing with. Cooper Cobb will not live past tomorrow night. I will make damn sure of it. I'm going to hit him where it hurts. It won't be the norm, though. This time it's different. This time, I take hostages. This time I will attempt to negotiate with him. If he doesn't agree to my terms, he will pay.

CHAPTER 57

COOPER COBB

"Welcome to this special live episode of the Knock Knock Podcast," I begin as I roll the intro music, "I'm your host, Cooper Cobb."

"And I'm Delilah Carney," says Delilah.

"Joining us for this special edition of the show is someone who has become an excellent friend to us and to the show; please welcome Tatum."

I watch as the listenership explodes. We took time to market the hell out of this episode in the previous twenty four hours. We want to make sure as many people are listening as humanly possible when we finally take him down.

10,000.

46,000.

93,000.

110,000.

208,000.

208,000 listeners and climbing, and we've only been live for a few minutes. I look over at Delilah; she is smiling with one of the biggest smiles I've ever seen on her face. She seems genuinely happy. She looks incredible. This is the most significant, most anticipated episode we've ever aired. Not only are we live on all of the major podcast networks, but we are also live streaming on YouTube and TikTok. We must ensure that as many people witness this as possible.

316,000 listeners now, and that doesn't include the live video streams. We are doing it. We are making it. This is it. This is our moment. The three of us look around at one another. Tatum's face lights up as she finally realizes how many people are listening and watching. Her hands begin to shake as the nerves fill her body, while Delilah and I simply can't contain our excitement as we stand at the microphones.

I look at Tatum and smile at her, and she shoots me a half-smile. She digs into her back pocket then pulls out her phone. We have particular rules for her, and one of the big ones is no phones while we are recording. I give her a disappointed look, but she is just staring at it, paying no attention to me. She locks it and sets it down on the table in front of her. It looks like she just received terrible news, but I try to ignore it.

"So, Tatum," I say into the microphone, "are you ready to tell your story?

Tatum lets out a big sigh, then says, "I'm ready."

"So this asshole," she says, pointing at me and smiling, "thought I was the killer."

My cheeks turn bright red upon hearing her say it out loud. The embarrassment I feel for the accusation is astounding. I'd prepared myself over and over for her to say it, but hearing it out loud is a different story.

"I'll spare you, listeners, the sexy details, but he was at my house…." She says.

As she says it, I look over at Delilah, who acts like she doesn't know we have been together intimately. She's looking away from us with a sad look on her face. I know it hurts her to hear it, and the last thing I ever want to do is destroy her emotionally. I'll make it up to her when this is all said and done.

As Tatum continues telling her story, an eerie feeling creeps over me. I'm not entirely sure what it is, but I briefly look over my shoulder as if I expected someone to be standing behind me, watching. It may just be because I know what we are about to do. I know who we are about to call out. His face is burned into my brain. The image of him creepily staring at me as he got out of my car. The unnerving feeling that he could have killed me then, but let me stew in my own thoughts.

Of course, no one is standing behind me. It's just the three of us in a studio. There's nowhere in the room where anyone could even hide. Tatum is wrapping up telling her tale, and I thank her for being on the show.

"Thank you for joining us to tell your story, Tatum, and again, I am so sorry for what I put you through," I say remorsefully. There is a brief silence from all three of us, then Delilah finally looks up at all of us.

"I'm sorry, too," she says, "for his dumbass."

All of us share a laugh for a moment.

506,000 listeners are now tuned in, and about 113,000 are watching the live streams.

"Should we take some calls now, you two?" I say.

"Let's do it," says Delilah. The two glance at each other as if they have something planned. I ignore it, though, and say, "Alright, the phone lines are open."

The phones start ringing off the hook. It's the usual song and dance; fans call in for a chance to say hi, tell us how much they love the show, and how much they are rooting for us to solve this problem. I think for a moment, then decide to say the one thing that has my anxiety through the roof.

"If Tom Langford is listening, call us," I say, "I'd love to chat with you."

The chat box goes absolutely nuts, and messages start scrolling so fast that I can't keep up with them. Delilah is standing across from me with her mouth wide open. I didn't tell her I was going to do it. I didn't tell her I was actually going to call him out. I look over at Tatum. Her face is similar to Delilah's, which, to me, is extremely weird. Why would she be so surprised by me calling out Tom?

What does she know?

CHAPTER 58

TOM LANGFORD

I'm sitting on the road on Route 113, waiting for the go-ahead. The sun is barely visible beyond the horizon, and the sky is filled with bright pinks, reds, and purples. I've never watched the sunset until now, but I can tell you it's one of the most peaceful things I've ever seen. I stare at it, and I can physically see it going down until it's no longer visible. The residual light is all that's left, and darkness begins to envelop the countryside.

I look out into the fields and see deer running toward the woods, trying to escape the darkness and hunker down for the evening. A little family of deer without a care in the world; a buck, a doe, and two fawns. It makes me think of the family I always wished I'd had. It's silly to compare my life to a herd of deer, but it's all I can think of.

The stars become visible, and I roll the driver's side window down and poke my head out. I'm observing them, trying to see if I can find any constellations. Finally, I spot the big dipper, probably the most common of all, but it's nice to look at. I can't say how long it's been since I looked up at the stars. My phone begins to vibrate while I'm enjoying some peace and quiet. I pick it up and look at it.

It's on.

I take a deep breath, get out of the car and go around to the back, sifting through the trunk to ensure I have everything I need. I grab my duffle bag, close the trunk, and saunter up the walkway. I reach the front door and knock twice, then kick the door so hard it cracks the frame and flies off the bottom hinge, hanging only by the top.

I stand in the doorway and look inside the home. I can see a man and a woman sitting in the living room, visibly shaken from the impact. The man stands up and looks at me while the woman is cowering in fear on the couch.

"What the fuck are you doing in our home?" He yells at me, "I'm giving you three seconds to get out of my house, or I'll shoot you."

I look at him and stare in deafening silence. I can see he's not holding a gun. I'm not scared of him. Fuck him. This man is a menace. I remember. I remember all the times he hit me. I remember all the times he locked me in my room. I remember when he told me I was a worthless piece of shit; he wished I was never born.

Oh, do I remember.

I stare, and he stares back. He starts to move toward me, and, with my hand behind my back and without saying a word, I reach in, grip, and point my gun at him.

"Knock, Knock, Dad," I say, then shoot him a sinister smile through the ski mask, pull the trigger, and shoot him in the leg, knocking him to the ground. Mom screams the highest-pitched, most blood-curdling scream I've ever heard.

CHAPTER 59
TOM LANGFORD

The couple gave me minimal struggle, surprisingly. I grabbed a couple of chairs from the kitchen and tied the two to them tight, avoiding any chance of escape. The home fell silent. No one spoke. The only sound I can hear is the sound of my own footsteps on the wood floor. I sit down in the worn-in recliner in the living room and stare at the two.

Mom is still crying, and Dad is staring at me from his position in the chair. I take off my mask and finally show them my face. They look at me like a complete stranger, but I know they know. I know they recognize me. They have to. They need to. Maybe they don't. It's been two decades since they left me at the fire station.

Finally, dad speaks up, breaking the silence that left all three of us feeling awkward.

"Who are you?" He says.

I project a thunderous, evil laugh as the words come out of his mouth. The question sounded sincere, though I can see on his face he is working through it, trying to solve the mystery. I stare at him for a few moments, then look back and forth between them.

"Tom?" Mom finally says, the tears drying to her cheeks now.

I smile at her instead of speaking, that same sinister smile I've grown accustomed to giving everyone.

"No," Dad says, "That's not Tom." He turns around, trying to look at his wife.

"It's me," I finally say, my tone much softer now, attempting to make them feel safe and secure.

I get up from the chair and start pacing back and forth next to them. Their eyes are following my every move. I look down and see blood still running from dad's leg. Not much, but enough. I can't let him bleed out, not yet.

I walk to the kitchen and get a towel, then back to Dad, bending down and tying the towel tight around his leg over the bullet hole. He winces as I pull and tighten. I imagine it stings; it hurts like a son of a bitch, but he doesn't say anything. I stand back up and stare at him.

"What do you want?" He says.

"Revenge," I say.

He stares at me as I walk over to my duffle bag, rummaging through to find a Bluetooth speaker I had packed for this moment. I pull it out and set it on the side table between the recliner and the couch. I pull out my phone and pull up a live feed from the YouTube account of Cooper's podcast. I set the phone up, leaning against the speaker on the table so they can see the entire feed. Tatum is talking about her experience of being taken into police custody and wrongly accused of my crimes. Well, mostly my crimes.

"This is about Cooper's podcast?" Dad says.

I reach my hand out and smack him hard across the face. The question made me see red. He doesn't get it. Neither one of them do.

"You don't get it, do you?" I scream at him as Mom starts crying again, harder this time.

The shocked look on his face is almost comical to me. The complete mix of confusion and rage shooting across his face makes me laugh. I'd never done it like this. I'd never put my victims through hell leading up to their deaths. There is something that feels good about it. I walk around in front of him, grabbing his face and coming almost nose to nose with him.

"You left me," I say, "you and this bitch." I gesture to my mom, and she starts sobbing even more.

"You left me alone at only seven years old with nothing. You didn't care, and neither did she. You left me to bounce around from foster home to foster home because you had a new baby. I was old news. I was trash. I was nothing to you. And that new baby? Well, clearly, he's the much more successful of the two of us." I gesture at the phone, still playing the live stream.

"Well, all three of you will die, but I'm going to make it last. I'm going to make it agonizing. I will watch you suffer and beg and plead for your life."

I wind up and punch him right on the nose. Blood starts trickling down his face.

"But not before I have a little fun with Cooper."

I stare at the phone and I hear Cooper say, "If Tom Langford is listening, call us, I'd love to chat with you." He knows. He knows who I am. He's figured it out. I smile a devious smile toward Mom and Dad. They look at me with fear striking them right in their hearts.

"Showtime," I say.

CHAPTER 60

COOPER COBB

Silence.

Dead silence.

None of us speak. Delilah is staring at me with her mouth wide open, as is Tatum, although I'm looking at her suspiciously. It seems she knows more than she is letting on. I shake the thought out of my mind, though. I look at Delilah and wink. She shakes her head and drops eye contact with me again, then quickly looks up at me, mouths, "I love you," and looks back down.

Even the phone lines are silent. Not a single person is ringing in. Our listeners and viewers are waiting on bated breath, waiting for something to go down. The chat is still blowing up, but the phone lines are silent. That's strange. That's not happened since our first live episode before we really blew up in popularity.

"Tom," I say again into the microphone, "if you are listening, call me. I want to talk to you."

Two minutes pass then the phone starts to ring, and I see Delilah and Tatum jump a little bit at the sound. I let it ring a couple of times as I come to the realization that this is real. This is happening. I didn't expect him to call at all, and even though I haven't answered yet, something in my gut tells me it's him. I answer the call.

"Y-you're on with Cooper, Delilah, and Tatum," I say with an audible shake in my voice; any confidence within me flew out the window as I answered the call.

"Knock, Knock, Cooper Cobb," the caller says.

"Hi, Tom," I say, attempting to radiate arrogance.

"Good job, you figured it out."

"I did."

"How's it feel that you were so close to death the other day? I could have killed you right then and there when you gave me that ride back home. How does it feel to know that?" Tom says threateningly.

"You're right. You could have," I say, "so why didn't you?"

The chat is scrolling even faster as people realize precisely who I'm talking to.

"No, Cooper, no," he says, "I wasn't going to off you right then. I felt compelled to fuck with you a little bit first."

I hear a scream mixed with the sound of frantic sobbing in the background of the call, then the sound of a smack and even harder crying. I know the tone of voice, but I can't place it; then I hear, "Cooper, don't be a hero," being yelled in the background, "give him whatever he wants."

My palms immediately get sweaty, my heart starts to race, and the world begins to spin around me. My eyes widen, and I place my hands on my head out of sheer panic and surprise. I know that voice, where he is, and who he has.

"Mom?" I say, "Dad?"

I fall into the chair behind me. I feel defeated, ambushed, and helpless from where I am. Luckily I have two others here with me. If we wanted to disconnect and cut the feed, we could. We could quickly run over to my parent's house, less than seven miles away. I'm currently carrying; we could be there in under five minutes. He wouldn't stand a chance.

I'm unable to speak. No matter how hard I try, I can't get anything to come out of my mouth. I stand back up and place my hands on the table. Think, Cooper, think, I say to myself. Suddenly, there is blinding pain on the backside of my cranium. Out of instinct, I reach back and place my hand on the back of my head. I feel wetness on my palm, and I take a look. Blood. The world begins to spin faster. Faster. Faster. I fall to the ground, and suddenly my vision goes black.

CHAPTER 61
COOPER COBB

Even with my eyes closed, the world is spinning. I can feel it. It's like going out drinking all night; even when you lay down and close your eyes, you have the spins. I start to come back, and it feels like I was out for hours. What hit me? My head is absolutely pounding; the worst headache I've ever had. I try to open my eyes, and it feels like there are weights on my eyelids. I can feel my pistol digging into the small of my back, held in place by my waistband.

As I open them, the world is a blur. I'm still in the studio, and I can make out the red glow of the sign on the wall that reads "Live." The show is still going. Did Tatum and Delilah keep things rolling after I fell to the ground and went unconscious? Why wouldn't they call for help? I blink my eyes repeatedly, and they begin to adjust. I can see shapes directly above me, and starting from the edge of my field of vision, things begin to clear up. I blink a few more times. With every blink, it feels like I'm factory resetting my sight.

When the clarity hits, I see Delilah and Tatum standing directly above me. Staring at me. They both look like they are about to kill me, then, in unison, suddenly, I have two pistols pointed at my face.

"Get up," Tatum says as she points the gun between my eyes. Neither of the girls is shaking, and it looks like they practiced this and planned for it. Steady does it. I reach up and grab onto the recording table to lift myself up. My head pounds as I stand.

"What are you doing?" I ask, confused. I look over at Delilah, "you?"

"Me," she says with a smirk, "it's always been me."

"Wait, wait, wait, so who is Tom?"

This is the last thing I expected. Delilah? Really? I missed it completely. I never suspected her of being involved with the killer. Tatum, however, makes sense. Mom and Dad. I hastily grab my headphones, throw them onto my ears, and yell into the microphone, "Mom? Dad?"

"They're still here. We all are," says Tom threateningly.

"Let me talk to them," I demand.

"We're here, son," the two of them say in unison. I sigh in relief.

I look over to the camera recording the live stream. It's still recording. The feed wasn't cut, and we are still live. I check the numbers, and we have over a million people now listening, and over a million and a half watching this all go down on social media. The shares are exploding. People are sharing the feed all across the world. I need to stay calm. This is my moment. All three of them may think they have me beat, but I'm determined to win.

I calmly motion for Delilah and Tatum to take their spots back at the microphones.

"For those of you listening, I'm going to urge you to head to YouTube or TikTok and watch the live stream so you can see what's going on in the studio right now," I say.

Suddenly, I watch as the number of listeners decreases rapidly and the number of viewers increases almost as fast. I've never been so thrilled to lose listeners, but they need to see who they are. They need to know them as I now know these two. Screw them. Whatever this ambush is, I'm going to kill them. I'm going to kill them all, and I'm going to save my parents. No matter what it takes.

With confused looks on their faces, the two girls take their places at the microphones. They don't say a word, but they continue to hold their firearms up and keep them pointed at me. They place their headphones back on but watch me like a hawk.

"Explain. Now," I demand, trying to keep my composure.

For a moment, no one speaks. No one looks like they're going to tell; then, through the headphones on the phone line, I hear Tom start to talk.

"I warned you, Cooper. I warned you to stop looking for me. I told you what would happen if you kept up the pursuit. You knew the consequences. Now, you're going to pay for it."

I always knew this, or something along these lines was a possibility. I didn't ever think, though, that he would go after my parents to get to me.

"Why don't you leave my parents out of this? It has nothing to do with them and everything with me."

"Oh, that's where you're wrong," he says, "this has everything to do with them."

I look up at Delilah, and she glances at Tatum, who doesn't notice and keeps her eyes locked on me.

"So tell me, Tom. What does this have to do with them?"

There is silence on the phone line, and I look around, first at Delilah again, then I turn to look at Tatum, though I end up looking down the barrel of her gun.

"Did your parents ever tell you," he starts, "that you have a brother?"

My heart sinks, and my eyes widen. My parents have never told me that I have a brother. No siblings. I always thought I was an only child. There were never any photos around the house; none I even stumbled on by accident.

"N-no," I say, "They haven't."

"Well, then, storytime," he says.

"Your parents have another son, and I am that son. I was born Thomas Andrew Cobb, and for the first seven years of my life, I was the love of theirs. I still hold the memories. I remember them playing with me; I remember playing catch in the front yard of the house I now stand in. I remember mom and her love for me. I remember it all. Everything was perfect.

"Then you came along. I remember I was six years old, and mom got pregnant with you. I was so excited to have a little brother, a little friend to play with, teach, and grow with. They say your siblings are your first best friends, and that's all I ever wanted us to be Cooper, but then you were born. Even as a seven-year-old child, I understood that the attention couldn't be on me completely and that you, this tiny little baby, needed much more attention. I was more self-sufficient and could handle being alone for a little while. It started as a few minutes here and there, then the minutes turned to hours, and the hours turned to days. I remember many moments of sitting in my room, lonely and unloved. I wasn't even retrieved for meals. I wasn't made aware there was food. I'd go days without eating, and I'd go days without speaking to them...."

My jaw dropped as Tom told his story. I had yet to learn about any of this. Of course, why would they tell me? They never treated me that way, and I always thought I had the best parents in the world. Now I'm starting to see that wasn't the case, especially as he continues his story.

"...then one day, mom came into my room and told me we were going for a drive, just the three of us. I grabbed my favorite stuffed bear, and we hit the road. We drove around for a while, and it felt so nice to hang out. I played with you while you were in your car seat, then, after a while, the car stopped, and I looked up and out the window, and I saw we were at the fire station. I was obsessed with fire trucks then, so you can imagine my excitement as mom told me to get out and that the firemen were waiting to show me around the big red vehicle. I got out of the car, and she told me she would park and bring you inside...."

I can hear my mom sobbing now. I can hear the regret in her sadness, even over the phone.

"...she drove away, and I remember walking inside the firehouse. The look on the firemen's faces when I walked in was that of surprise and confusion. They asked me what I was there for, and I told them my mom had dropped me off and she was just parking the car before she came inside. I told them I was there for them to show me the firetruck. I remember the looks on their faces, and they ran to the door and saw mom driving off. They weren't quick enough to get her license plate and I didn't know my own address. I could see the taillights on her car; they were gone the next moment. She was gone. You were gone. Never to be seen again."

I'm at a loss for words. There's nothing I can say to make things better or go back in time and stop her from doing what she did.

"So," I say, "why the killing?"

"Jealousy," he says, "jealousy of what others have that I didn't, fueled by pure rage."

"Now, I'm here to get my revenge. Revenge on you and them. Revenge on the people that sent me out into the cold world by myself at a young age. Fuck you, Cooper, and fuck them too."

I'm left with more questions than answers. I know his story and his motivations, but I don't know why or how he dragged Delilah and Tatum into this. Tatum is one thing, but Delilah, I don't know if I want to learn the answer, but he gives it to me anyway as if he is reading my mind.

"Oh, and your friends there, Delilah and Tatum?" He starts, "Tatum approached me herself. She wanted to be involved. She hates you, Cooper. She thinks you're sticking your nose into business that doesn't concern you. Her hate for you is what drove her to join me."

I look over at Tatum and she smiles deviously as Tom tells me her motivations. Her hatred for me was so intense that she killed people. She killed people to get to me. It served as a warning; a warning that I ignored. It was all a lie. The short relationship we had was a lie.

"So what? The sex was…" I say.

"A fucking lie, Cooper. God, you're an idiot." She says. "I hate you. I hate you so much. You drove me to kill, but Tom—Tom guided me. He taught me the ways. He showed me how to kill and how good it feels to take another life. God, it's a rush."

She presses the gun to my head, and I close my eyes tightly, waiting for the shot to go off and for everything to end.

"What about the knife in your room?" I ask. I need to know.

"Ha! That?" She says, "Tom got pissed at me for no reason and he thought he would get back at me and frame me for everything, but when I got out of police custody, and they couldn't charge me for the murders, he knew I was valuable. I knew it was there the whole time, and I knew you would find it, Cooper. You're observant. I'll give you that."

She presses the gun to my head even harder now, so hard, in fact, that she just about pushes me over. She wants to pull the trigger, but I can feel a slight shake in her hand. She tightens her grip on the firearm, and a muscle flexes in her arm. I close my eyes as I fully expect her to pull the trigger.

"Tatum, don't," says Tom, "not yet. Don't forget, I can see you. It's not time yet. Cooper deserves to know every last detail."

I look over at Delilah, and her hand is still pointing the gun out at me. The look on her face tells me she's ashamed that she joined them and regrets it. I can see her hand trembling now as the nerves take over.

"Delilah Rae," Tom says, "my other love." I can hear the smile in his voice, and my hand balls up into a fist unintentionally as if I'm going to punch him through the phone. The rage I feel with him using her middle name is a little excessive, but then again, everything else going on at the present time is also outrageous.

"I came to her," he continues, "I needed an inside look at your life. I needed to know everything you were doing and when you were doing it. I needed to keep tabs on you, Cooper. This wouldn't work if I didn't know everything. Who knew all it took for a lifelong friend to abandon someone was a little bit of money."

The smile in his voice becomes larger. I can hear it. That broad smile is maddening. I look back up at Delilah, and redness fills her cheeks. I can see her embarrassment, and I can almost feel it myself. I missed literally every sign and every red flag, though; both of these bitches are great actresses and they were able to avoid me finding out everything, and for that, I can applaud them.

I look at Delilah and say, "how much?"

She sighs. I know she doesn't want to tell me, but I need to know.

"$250,000," she says.

"$250,000?" I exclaim, "shit, I can't blame you; I'd ditch your ass for a quarter of a million too!"

The three of us laugh together, though it's not funny, dark humor will get us through this. But I know what I'm going to have to do, and I know I won't like it. It's not going to feel good, but I know I will have to kill my best friend if I'm ever going to get out of this. Out of nowhere, a gunshot goes off on the other end of the phone.

"Shut up, shut up," Tom yells at us, "nothing about this is funny."

We stop laughing, and I listen intently, trying to figure out whether that is a warning shot or real, silently hoping someone watching the live stream calls the police, though, they're probably too entertained.

"Did you," I say, "...did you kill one of them?"

"Not yet, but soon I will."

How am I going to get out of this? How am I going to beat him at his own game? It's two against one right now. I must find a way out of the studio and get to my parents before it's too late. My eyes dart around the room as I devise a game plan.

BANG!

Another gunshot goes off, and my ears ring as if a grenade went off next to me. Instinctively, my hands grab onto my torso, and I bring myself back to reality. I wasn't shot. Not me. I look up, and I see Delilah standing there. The end of her gun is smoking, and I look to my left. Tatum isn't there, but behind where she was standing, a bright splotch of crimson is splattered on the wall. I'm surprised YouTube hasn't taken the stream down yet, but it might be time to switch to our backup account. I look down to see her body on the ground, a bullet hole blown right into the side of her head. I look back up at Delilah.

"Let's go save your parents," she says.

CHAPTER 62

COOPER COBB

We are in Delilah's bright pink Volkswagen, flying down Route 113 and heading to my parent's house. I am hoping and praying we aren't too late. We know that Tom saw her kill his only faithful accomplice; for all we know, they could be dead by the time we show up, and he could be long gone. My whole body shakes with anxiety; it feels like my life's longest, most grueling drive.

"I was never going to kill you, just so you know," Delilah says to me, "never in a million years."

"I know," I say, "I'll admit it was a shock to find out you were involved with him, but—" She cuts me off.

"I did it for one reason and one reason only," she says, "to protect you."

"I'm sure the money was pretty beneficial, too," I say.

She chuckles. If we get out of this alive, we will be set. We can move forward. I can forgive her, and I hope we can start our life together as a couple. For the last few days, she and I together was all I could think about. I love her, and I love her even more now. She will always be there for me, and I know I can return the favor, but hopefully not in this capacity. No, I shake the thought out of my mind. This ends tonight. After tonight no more fucking Tom Langford and no more fucking Knock Knock Killer.

I pull the gun out of the back of my waistband, and Delilah looks at me, shocked. I cock the gun and set it on the dash for a moment. I check my shoes, making sure they're tied tight. Nothing can go wrong; everything has to be precise for this to go over well. We are going in completely blind, and we don't know what we will find, and we also have absolutely no plan.

I pull out my phone, pull up the YouTube app, and navigate our channel. It's the best I can do, and I don't know how I'm going to do it, but we owe it to our viewers and listeners to be witness to the moment we finally take him down. I don't know where this arrogance has come from, but I think I will need as much of a cocky attitude as I can muster to pull this off.

I hit the "Go Live" button on the app, and it fills with viewers quickly.

14,000.

70,000.

169,000.

The viewership continues to grow as people abandon our previous live stream for this one. I have to say something. I have to tell them what's going on. They all saw it go down in the studio before I knew what had happened, but I need to update them quickly.

"If you are watching this, then you know Delilah and I are okay. Here's the update: She was never truly involved with him. She joined forces with the Knock Knock Killer to protect me, and I am eternally grateful to her for that. We are currently—"

I stop myself. If Tom is watching, he can't know we are on our way. He can't know we are prepared to take him down now.

"...just know that we are okay. I will keep this stream going as long as possible, but I don't know how much time we have left. I'll try to keep it steady and keep you all informed. If you are watching this, please send us prayers, and good vibes, whatever you do. We will need everything you've got to send our way," I say.

279,000.

405,000.

942,000.

We pass by my parent's house. He can't even know that we are there, we need to take him completely by surprise, but as we roll by, I can see him pacing inside, and I catch a quick glimpse of my parents. It looks like they are still alive, tied to a couple of kitchen chairs. We pull down the road and park, turning the vehicle off and waiting for a moment.

"You ready?" I say.

"Yes," says Delilah, pulling out her gun and cocking it, putting a bullet in the chamber.

I lean over and kiss her. I've never seen her so sexy. Something about her holding a gun has me very excited. I have to block the thoughts from my mind. I have to focus. We need to focus.

"This ends now," I say as I exit the car and slam the door.

CHAPTER 63

COOPER COBB

We are running through the barren corn fields making our way back to the house, the mud underneath our feet squishing as we make our way through the mess. We can hear coyotes howling in the distance, so we know that's a risk. Luckily, we have our firearms so we can protect ourselves. We must conserve ammunition, though, so I hope we don't have any issues.

Delilah is about ten steps ahead of me, and she catches her foot on a rut in the ground and tumbles forward, rolling as she hits the ground. I can see the silhouette of her gun go flying through the air in the dim moonlight hidden behind some thick clouds. I run up to her and hold out my hand, which she grabs hastily as I pull her back to her feet. I grab my phone and it doesn't take long to find the gun, which she grabs and immediately begins running again.

In the slight distance between us and the house, we can see the light shining through the windows so we know we are close. We take a moment to catch our breath so we can keep moving. We can't be too worn out before we get there. The battle hasn't begun yet. We grab one another's hand and stand staring at the sky. At this moment, it's just the two of us, and I wish it could last forever. I wish we weren't there for the reason that we are. No stars are visible and, as we look toward the heavens, a raindrop hits me directly in the eye. We can see the flash of lightning and hear the thunder in the distance. There would be a storm rolling in right now, I think, though it is pretty appropriate.

We make it to the property line between the field and my parent's house, hiding behind a massive tree blocking us from view. Though the darkness should hide us reasonably well, we can't take chances. We peek around, and I see my parents through the window, still tied to the chairs. I see them moving, so he's spared them so far. I can see Tom pacing back and forth in front of them, and it looks like he's trying to devise a plan. He didn't plan for Delilah defecting on him. He thought he had every second planned. My bond with her is more valuable than any amount of money can buy.

I look Delilah in the eyes, move her hair out of her face and brush it behind her ear. I place the palm of my hand on her cheek, and she grabs my hand with hers. I want this moment to last. I watch as a tear rolls down her face and I wrap my fingers around the back of her head, pulling her in close and resting my forehead on hers. I kiss her forehead and look her deep in the eyes.

"I love you, Delilah Rae Carney," I say, "I always will."

"I love you, too," she says.

"No matter what happens tonight, no matter where I am, just remember, I'll always be with you. Always."

She smiles at me and then says, "Same, but you and I? We are going to get through this. We will be together when this is over. I promise."

She plants a big kiss on my lips, then I peek around the tree again. Tom's back is turned to the front door. It's now or never.

"Okay. I've got it. Here's the plan," I say.

CHAPTER 64
COOPER COBB

I'm standing just outside the front door. It's hanging just barely by the top hinge. I double-check to make sure I have a round in the chamber of my Glock 43; there is. I pat around on my waist to make sure the Buck 119 is still in its sheath; it is. I'm set and ready to go. I listen intently to see if I can hear what Tom is saying. It's primarily inaudible, but I can tell he's starting to lose his mind. I can hear him slamming around in the kitchen, meaning my parents are left unattended. I peek around the corner, and my dad makes eye contact with me. I hold a single finger up to my mouth to make sure he keeps quiet.

Delilah is around the corner of the house, keeping tabs on things from a different angle. She's more of a lookout than anything. I asked her to just watch and only come inside if it looked like I needed help. If it gets awful, she knows to call the cops. I look through the living room and past my parents. I can see her head poking up just above the windowsill.

I hear footsteps approaching the living room, so I back off just slightly so that I am out of sight but can still see inside. I watch as Delilah drops to the ground so she isn't spotted. Tom walks by holding a frying pan and approaches my father. He looks at him thoughtfully, then holds the pan up.

"Where is he?" He yells at my dad, shaking his head.

"I don't know." My dad says.

Thanks, Dad, but dammit.

I hear the smack of the frying pan as Tom swings it and smokes Dad in the head. I peek in to get a better look to check his status. He's sitting there with his head hanging down, and blood is dripping from his nose and mouth. He spits and a tooth goes flying onto the floor. Tom lets out a roaring laugh at the sight of him spitting his tooth out.

He walks around to Mom, and I gulp out of fear. I can see Delilah sneaking a look as her head raises ever so slightly. Tom pulls out his own Buck 119 and holds it to her throat. My grip tightens on the Glock as I consider running in now, but it's not perfect. My timing needs to be perfect. Based on his actions so far, he isn't going to make a move yet. I can barely hear him, but I can hear him threatening her life. Then he pulls the knife away, raises it, and slams the blade down into her thigh. Delilah winces in the window. I observe as he removes the knife, looking for any signs that he hit the femoral artery. Blood drips to the floor, but not enough to have hit it, thankfully.

He turns around and fires a round out of his gun into the television, and glass flies all over the room. He runs over to it and, in a fit of rage, grabs it and rips it down from the wall causing it to crash to the floor. He almost looks like a five-year-old throwing an absolute fit because his mom told him no for the first time. He overturns furniture in his rage.

It's almost time. Tom is losing it because he can't see where I am. I can see that he's getting nervous. For once, someone other than him is in control. Unfortunately, it means that soon I will need to make an appearance. Soon I will need to come out of hiding. I'm not ready for it, but if I don't, if I let my nerves get the best of me and I stay hidden, both of my parents will die. He could get away, and we won't accomplish what we came here for.

I reach down and check my phone. I have it secured in my pocket with the top half sticking out so that everyone can see what's happening. Everyone needs to see it, and they need to know. Whether they're original fans, new fans, or people watching for the first time doesn't matter. The Knock Knock Podcast will go down in history as the most immersive podcast ever.

Tom slowly walks over to Mom and presses his gun to her head. Pushing so hard, in fact, that he is tipping her just enough to lift one side of the chair she is sitting in off its legs. I now grip the Glock harder and can feel my knuckles turning white.

"That's it," Tom yells, "this ends now."

I step out of hiding and am face to face with the man we have been hunting for months. He looks up and sees me, and we stare at one another for a minute. Dad looks up and sees me, and for the first time in a long time, I see a smile flash across his face. I see Delilah in the window and her jaw drops; even though she knows this would happen, it's as if she doesn't realize it was part of the plan. I look at him and he looks at me. He seems taken off guard and pulls the gun from Mom's head, grabs her chair, and throws her to the ground.

"You want me, not them," I say, "well, come on. Shoot me, motherfucker."

Though I can't hear her, I can read Delilah's lips through the window as she yells, "No." He stares at me with that ugly-ass, evil smile, and I can see the gears turning in his mind. He's waited for this moment. He's planned for this moment, though I can see a shred of hesitation in his body language.

"Cooper," he says calmly, "nice of you to join us."

A moment of silence falls within the house, then he says, "Now I can kill all four of you at once."

He looks over his shoulder, acknowledging that he knew Delilah was there the entire time, or at least he wants us to think that.

CHAPTER 65

COOPER COBB

As I move closer, I have my gun raised and pointed directly at Tom's head. I'm a good shot, but I'm not that good; I need to be in closer proximity. I move slowly and deliberately as I close the gap between us. The tension in the room rises, and I can feel my body wanting to start shaking like a leaf, but I regain control of the involuntary muscle spasms.

Delilah is still watching us through the window, and I jerk my head back as a sign for her to come inside while still keeping a close eye on Tom. He doesn't look like he wants to fight back and hasn't raised his gun toward me or charged me with his knife. Just nothing. It's not exactly the big showdown I was expecting; truth be told, I wasn't entirely sure what to expect.

Delilah walks inside with her gun drawn, pointing at Tom as well. There we are, just the two of us about to take down the most notorious serial killer in Ohio. I don't know how I expected it to feel, but it wasn't like this. It could be that I just found out he is my long-lost brother, though that doesn't change my opinion too much. I'm still going to kill him. I'm still going to watch as the light leaves his eyes. He will never kill again.

I look over briefly to check on Dad, and Tom has closed the gap between us just slightly. He is almost even with Dad's spot in the chair, standing right next to him. I can see Dad wiggling, just barely trying to escape the ropes that have him held into place. He's going to try to be a hero. I know he wants to. Tom turns for a brief second to grab the phone he has set up sitting on the side table, and while his attention is on that, I look at Dad and shake my head. He stops trying to escape.

Tom is messing around on the phone, then he smiles, turns it around, and shows me the image on the screen. He is showing me my point of view from the camera in my pocket. He knew I would be live streaming this.

"Don't want to disappoint your viewers," he says. Delilah and I exchange a look. "It's okay. I want them to see the moment I kill you."

"That's where you're wrong," I say, "because, at the end of this, you're the one who will be dead."

He laughs at me mockingly. He's arrogant and has a god complex so strong that he doesn't think he can be killed or stopped. He still sees this as a typical murder, and though the process has been drawn out, he still feels that he will be the winner at the end of the day. I take a couple of steps toward him, closing the gap even more until I face him. I raise the gun and put it to his head. My dad looks at me with fear, and for a moment, I take my sights off of him just long enough.

A piercing, screaming pain shoots through my abdomen. It's white hot and feels like I'm being cut open from end to end. I can feel it through my entire body and, despite my best efforts, I attempt to grip the Glock in my hand, but it falls and clatters to the ground. I look down and see his Buck knife sticking out of my left side; Tom reaches up and puts a hand on my shoulder, then digs the blade in deeper, causing tears to run from my eyes.

"I told you," he says, "I will kill you."

He rips the knife from my body, and blood begins to run out of the open wound. I put my hand down and grab on, applying as much pressure as possible. I think I'll be okay. He stayed far enough to the left and didn't go too deep. I'm okay, I'm okay, I think. The pain causes me to fall to the ground, and I lay on the floor, clutching my side, feeling almost too helpless to get back up. I look up at dad, and he smiles at me, mouthing the words, "You've got this."

I pull myself back up off the hardwood floor and look at him. I can see the satisfaction in his eyes. The never-ending arrogance that this man exudes is astonishing.

"You," I say with a struggle, "are no brother of mine. After this is over, you will be left with nothing. Just like you were when you were left at that fire station."

The cocky smile fades from his face, and he yells with a ferocity that makes me jump, lifting the blade up in preparation to swing it back down and end everything. That comment. That one single comment was the straw that broke the camel's back. As he swings the blade down to stab me again, I throw my hands up and…

BANG! BANG!

Two gunshots ring through the air, and suddenly Tom is on the ground. I look over at Delilah, and the barrel of her gun is smoking again. She shot him. She shot him twice. I look over at him as blood drips onto the floor. She shot him in the leg, not enough to kill, but to wound him and to slow him down. He gets up and runs with a limp out of the house. He knows he is no match for us now. I look at Delilah, and she is smiling with satisfaction on her face.

"Why the legs?" I ask her.

"I couldn't kill him," she says, "I want you to have that satisfaction."

We make our way over to my parents; I go to Dad and she to Mom. She lifts mom up off the floor, and I start untying my dad. The four of us remain silent until they are free of their binds. The two of them grab onto the other and hold one another for what feels like forever. Then Dad looks at me and says, "go, you two. Go finish what you started."

CHAPTER 66

COOPER COBB

Back on the road in the bright pink Volkswagen, we are speeding down Route 113, and I can see the taillights on Tom's car in the distance, maybe a half mile down the road. Delilah is pushing the upper limits of what her tiny four-cylinder vehicle can take. The front is shaking so hard that it feels like the tires are about to fly off into the fields, leaving us stranded and letting him get away.

Still, we are catching up with him. Luckily, her car is a little newer and can withstand the stress she puts it under easier than his car can. I'm white-knuckling the 'oh shit' handle as we fly down the road. A quarter mile away from him now. Delilah has her foot pressed to the floor, and I don't think it can handle much more.

We are right on him now, tailgating him. He swerves to get us off his tail, but Delilah is driving in a way I've never seen before. She's going as if she is at the Indy 500 and about to push past the car in front of her into first place. She glances at me briefly. She has an idea, but I can also tell that it's risky. I grab the handle tighter as I brace myself for whatever she has planned.

Suddenly, she swerves into the other lane right into oncoming traffic, though at this time of night in our small town, no one is out driving, so at least that risk is minimized. She looks at me again, and now I know her plan. She pushes the gas slightly harder and barely gets her hood even with his trunk. She looks at me and says, "Hold on tight," then swerves to the left, then hard to the right, barely clipping the back left of his rear bumper.

His car spins out of control and then slides into a ditch. The impact sends the car flying off into a wooded area as it flips five times, then lands on its passenger side. Delilah slams on the brakes and looks for a way to drive back to his vehicle. We find a small driveway and pull down it to get as close as we can. As we pull up, Tom pulls himself out of the driver's side, knife and gun in hand. She shines her high beams to blind him momentarily while we get out of the vehicle.

We look around, observing our surroundings. All we can see is whatever is in front of the car, illuminating the landscape. We see stones all around us in various shapes and sizes. Headstones. A cemetery? That's appropriate.

"This ends now, Tom," I yell as he throws himself to the ground. He looks around and realizes where we are as well.

"You're right," he says, "and how fitting. The funeral home won't have to take you two very far."

He charges at us, using any last bit of energy he has to try to take us down. I push Delilah out of the way and tell her to run and call the police. I need backup. I need help. She does as she's told. He runs at me and tackles me to the ground, and we roll around for a minute, both of us swinging at the other, trying to get the upper hand.

The two of us stand up and stare at one another, and just as I'm about to pull out my gun, raise it, and shoot him between the eyes, a silhouette catches my eye, charging in out of the darkness. Tom doesn't notice and gets tackled back to the ground. Who is that? I think. I strain my eyes, trying to make out the figure, but they are moving too quickly for me to catch a glimpse. Then they move just enough back into the light of the headlights, and I can see who it is.

"Riley?" I yell.

CHAPTER 67
COOPER COBB

I'm left speechless as I stand and stare at Riley, dumbfounded by how he knew where to find us. It doesn't make sense, so I reach down and touch my pocket. My phone is still sticking out, live streaming everything. Riley is fighting Tom, trying to keep him down, though Tom seems amused. I can see him in the dim light, not fighting back but laughing. Riley lands a massive punch with an audible thud to the face, making Tom laugh harder.

I walk up to help him restrain Tom, and that's when he fights back harder. He grabs Riley by his sides and launches him off of him, throwing him a good five feet, then jumps back to his feet as Riley does the same. He immediately pulls out his gun and points it at me. Riley runs to my side as we stand and stare at Tom, still cackling.

I can hear the thunder and see the lightning getting closer to us; it's about to storm. Rain begins to drop from the sky harder and harder every second until the three of us are standing there soaking wet, the dirt on our clothes turning into mud.

"Why are you laughing," I ask Tom as he continues to laugh, almost unable to catch his breath to give us a word.

"Look around," he says finally, "look around you. Do you know where you are?"

We look around and observe. I can tell we are in the cemetery, but not entirely sure what he's getting at. I start to notice the names on the headstones, and it occurs to me. We are in the newer part of the cemetery where the more recently passed are buried.

A couple of years ago, the city decided to dedicate an area of the cemetery to the victims of the Knock Knock Killer, and, with the permission of the families, the bodies were exhumed and moved to the newly constructed memorial. Every single victim of Tom Langford is buried in one specific place. It's appropriate that this is where he will die. I'm determined to make it happen. It's a sweet sort of justice.

Riley's face drops as he makes the same realization I did, just a little slower. He looks at me with anger in his eyes and his hair dripping wet. I can see his fists ball up and notice he came very unprepared. No weapon at all. I hand him my knife, so he isn't entirely without self-defense measures.

Without notice, I raise my gun and point it at Tom, and he does the same with his. We are standing in the pouring rain in the middle of a cemetery waiting for the other to pull the trigger like we are in some sort of western-style shootout.

"This ends now, Tom," I yell over a crack of thunder.

"Yes, it does," he says.

I pull the trigger, and a flash of lightning fills the cemetery simultaneously. Tom drops to the ground and drops his gun as the bullet rips through his shin. He's going to suffer. He's going to feel what every single one of his victims felt. I'm going to make him beg for death.

The two of us walk up to him, and Riley kicks the gun out of his reach. He looks up at me with wide, scared eyes. I fire off another shot into his other leg. He kicks and squirms in agonizing pain. I can feel the fire in my soul, and now I know how he feels when he kills. I can feel the adrenaline coursing through my veins. I've never felt as close to this man as I do now.

Luckily, Riley doesn't have to use the knife I handed him, so I grab it back and bend down to be face-to-face with Tom. I can hear sirens in the distance. Too little too late, but she did it. She got them to come, but they're coming to retrieve nothing more than a dead body by the time they get here.

Another crack of thunder rings through the air, and a flash of lightning illuminates everything. I look up at Riley, though I shouldn't be taking my eyes off Tom.

"Riley, get out of here. I told you I wouldn't involve you," I say.

"I got myself involved. I couldn't let you go it alone."

"Riley, go," I bark at him. He takes off into the darkness.

I look back to Tom, and he squeezes his eyes shut tightly. I can assume it's because of the pain in his legs. I dramatically raise the knife in my right hand, as you would see in a slasher movie. I imagine the cameraman showing a close-up of the blade in my hand as another flash of lightning cracks across the night sky. I swing the knife down and stab directly into his abdomen, just below his sternum. He coughs and gags as the blade rips through his flesh. I pull it out quickly, and his eyes widen.

"Brother, don't," he says pleadingly.

I raise the knife and swiftly swing it back down, stabbing him lower now, ripping through his intestines. Blood doesn't pour out, though, as I expected it to. Gravity keeps it in as he lies on the ground. I slash the blade through his flesh, widening the opening. He coughs and gags more as blood starts to fly out of his mouth. I rip the knife out again.

"You're no brother of mine," I say as I hold the knife to his throat.

Just then, I hear footsteps sloshing in the mud behind me. I turn around to see Delilah reappearing, her hair plastered to her face from the rain. She reaches up and moves it out of her eyes. She's begging me without saying anything to stop now. This is torture, I know it is, but this man deserves to suffer. He deserves to die a slow and painful death, and he is. As we live and breathe, he is. His breathing is slowing down as he coughs up more blood. He attempts to speak, but can no longer form coherent words and it just comes out as babbling. I look at Delilah, and she knows I will do it. She knows I'm going to finish the job. I place the knife to his throat with a threatening look in my eyes as I stare deep into his. They are again begging me not to do what he knows is coming. I grip the knife tighter and look down at the handle for a moment. Sweet revenge, death by his own blade as I remember I'm carrying the one with the "T.L." engraved at the bottom of the it. I remove it from his throat, placing it in front of him so he can see it and though it comes out as a gurgle, he chuckles lightly. He grabs my hand, then moves the serrated edge back to his throat. I grip it tight, then slide it width-wise across his throat, making sure to hit the carotid artery.

The coughing and gagging intensify as blood pours out of his neck. His eyes widen as he tries to breathe, but he can't get any sort of decent breath into his lungs. I stand and back up to Delilah as he slowly dies. She reaches her pinky over and touches my hand. I grip hers tightly. Tom finally gets a deep breath in, then lets it out.

No more breathing, no more writhing in pain, but just to be sure, I raise the gun and, without hesitation, shoot him in the head. For only a moment, we stand and admire our work, though that sounds a little messed up.

So, here I stand, gun in hand, drenched with rain and body fluids. Blood, mostly, I think, but who knows; I don't even know whose blood is on me. Is it mine? The scuffle was intense, though scuffle is a gentle way to explain it. It was the worst thing I'd ever experienced in my life. But it was done and over with.

So many questions are running through my mind, but the biggest one is: what did I do to deserve this? I don't think I was the target. I would have never been on the radar, but I kept digging and digging. I kept searching. I needed an answer, and in the worst way possible, I got it.

As I stand here, out of breath, heart racing in the pouring rain, she grabs my hand even harder. I drop the gun on the ground, and she looks me in the eyes.

"It's over," she says, "You won."

"We won," I say to her.

CHAPTER 68

COOPER COBB

The rain begins lightening up as we stand around with police officers, detectives, and crime scene investigators. They surround the cemetery with yellow tape, and the forensic photographer is there snapping photos of Tom's lifeless body before the medical examiner shows up. We are being questioned by police, trying to get a complete picture of what happened.

Luckily, they're very calm about everything and are letting us sit in the back of an ambulance at the paramedic's request so they can check us out. The air around us is starting to cool down, and with our clothes soaked, it feels much colder than it is. The paramedics bring a shock blanket to keep us warm, and we wrap up together. Delilah is resting her head on my shoulder, and for once, the world feels peaceful other than the chaos around us. I ignore it, though. It's just her and I.

I dig my phone out of my pocket, fully expecting it to be shut down with water damage, but it's not, and the stream is still going. I click the button to flip the camera around and show our faces. I look right into the camera, and Delilah looks up at me.

"What are you going to say to them?" she asks.

I think about it and stare at the scene before us. I smile. I look back to the phone and see over 4,000,000 viewers still hanging in to witness the end of our harrowing adventure. I turn my head, kiss the top of hers, and then look back into the camera.

"This has been the Knock Knock Podcast with Cooper Cobb," I say, then, without missing a beat, she says, "...and Delilah Carney."

I hit the button to stop the stream, put my phone away, and wrap my arms around her. My world is complete. I caught the killer, killed the killer, and got the girl. What more could a guy in my position ask for?

SIX MONTHS LATER

CHAPTER 69
COOPER COBB

It's been six months since we took down the Knock Knock Killer A.K.A Tom Langford, A.K.A. Thomas Andrew Cobb. I say "we" because if it wasn't for the help of Riley and Delilah, there's no way we could have done it. The media constantly reminds me that I am the one that took him down, but I don't like that kind of attention. It was a group effort and always will be in my mind.

The three of us are sitting at the coffee shop, laughing and joking, having a great time. After we took him down, for a while, things were busy for Delilah and me. We were interviewed on so many different television specials like Good Morning America and The Late Show With Jimmy Fallon, just to name a couple. This is the first time in six months that we can breathe freely. The interviews have slowed down, and now we only do a couple here and there for the stragglers over Zoom mostly.

Delilah and I made things official right after, and we've been happily dating ever since. I feel bad for Riley, though. He helped and got himself mixed up in it even though he said he never would, but no one knows, except the two of us, that he was even there that night in the cemetery. Though I feel bad, he likes it that way. He doesn't want the attention or the hassle like we've had to deal with.

My phone starts to ring, and I look at the screen. It's Detective Carpenter. I answer it.

"Hello, this is Cooper," I say.

This is the first time I've spoken to him since the morning he was at our house and I handed over all of our evidence. The police never came up with anything. They were always empty-handed. I still don't trust them to solve any cases, but for him to reach out to me, it's a nice gesture.

He goes into an extensive explanation, thanks me for everything we did, and even admits that they had no idea what they were doing. Still, they are happy we were on it, but he reminds me to come straight to them if we ever run into a situation like that again. They don't want average everyday citizens getting mixed up in someone's crime, which makes sense to me. I thank him for his call.

With the podcast ending, we have a lot of free time these days, though we have more listeners than ever. We negotiated with YouTube to keep the original live stream up so that new people finding us can follow the story to the end. They agreed under the condition that we blur certain parts, which we gladly obliged.

Delilah is in the middle of writing a book about the whole ordeal. Personally, I've decided to leave it behind me. I don't need to do anything to make money for now. We are still sitting pretty from the money Tom gave to Delilah and the ad revenue that continues coming in from the show. She felt the need to write a book to give her some closure. It started with her therapist telling her to write her thoughts on paper to get them out of her mind, but now it's grown more significant. She has some large publishers keeping an eye on her new book titled The Podcast: How an Internet Show Took Down a Notorious Serial Killer. It has definitely helped her in the grieving process.

What will I do now? I don't know yet. For now, I'm going to chill and enjoy life. I've got my two best friends, and my parents are still alive. I couldn't ask for much more. I've been planning, though, and I think the next step is even scarier than facing the Knock Knock Killer, because, at the end of the day, he was nothing more than an average guy. I look at Delilah and admire everything about her image; her hair, eyes, and skin. She looks over and catches me staring, and the lightest pink touches her cheeks. I'm going to marry this girl, I think. I've got the ring; I'm just waiting for the right time.

ACKNOWLEDGEMENTS

There are so many people that I want to thank that had something to do with the writing of this book. A lot of heart and soul went into the creation of this work and I greatly hope you've enjoyed it. A lot of people worked their tails off to make this a success. No person in this list of acknowledgements is in any particular order.

First and foremost, I need to thank my wife, Ashley Thomas. Thank you for everything. You are my rock and a massive inspiration for my creative side (especially when I'm writing about serial killers). You are absolutely everything in the world to me and I wouldn't have been able to do this without you. Thank you for dealing with all of my wacky ideas. You know when I get an idea, it's best to back off and simply say "sounds good, babe!"

Secondly, I need to give thanks to my children, Sophia and Asher. Dad spent a lot of time sitting and staring at his laptop to write this and when I was doing that, both of you understood and left me to my work without bothering me. You two are the light of my life and I can't imagine living without you.

Next, a thank you to my mom for raising me into the man I am today and always supporting everything I do.

Next up, a huge shoutout to my best friend Cody Scaramuzzino for being everything a best friend should be and supporting me in a similar fashion to Ashley. I get a little crazy sometimes, but you've always been by my side.

Next, I'd like to thank Samantha Semerau. Thank you for your hard work and dedication in editing and proofreading this work. I know you are going to do fantastic things in life and in your career. Thank you for dealing with all of my BS everytime I told you I added another chapter, or I made changes to something you already edited.

Next, a huge shout out goes to rebecacovers on Fiverr for creating an amazing paperback and ebook cover for this work. Also to cyber_avanza on Fiverr for creating some promotional material for me.

Lastly, a thank you goes out to the late Wes Craven who inspired my love for all things horror and suspense at the age of six when I watched Scream for the first time.

MORE TITLES BY STEVEN T. THOMAS

Who's There? (Knock Knock Series Book 2)
Guess Who (Knock Knock Series Book 3)

www.ingramcontent.com/pod-product-compliance
Lightning Source LLC
Chambersburg PA
CBHW010427120726
47992CB00010B/3350